Llyfrgell Ceredigion
Ceredigion Library

SHERLOCK HOLMES AND THE QUEEN OF DIAMONDS

When Thomas Howard of Missouri had come out of nowhere, one foggy night, and rescued Countess Elaina Montague from rape and robbery, he was apparently in England to find his brother who had disappeared. The Countess offered to enlist Sherlock Holmes to help Howard in his search, though he was already investigating a rash of audacious jewel-thefts. However, the Great Detective, suspecting that there was more to Mr Howard than met the eye, accepted the case. This led to their involvement in a vicious blood feud, a spectacular — death-defying — daylight robbery and a thrilling climax below the brooding River Thames.

D1407502

Books by Steve Hayes & David Whitehead
Published by The House of Ulverscroft:

FERAL
DEAD END
FANATICS
KILLER SMILE
UNDER THE KNIFE
CAST A DEADLY SHADOW
TOMORROW, UTOPIA
BLACKOUT!
COMES A STRANGER

By Steve Hayes:
GUN FOR REVENGE
A WOMAN TO DIE FOR
VIVA GRINGO!
PACKING IRON
A COFFIN FOR SANTA ROSA
TRAIL OF THE HANGED MAN

By David Whitehead:
HELLER
STARPACKER
TRIAL BY FIRE
HELLER IN THE ROCKIES
THE FLUTTERING
SCARE TACTICS

STEVE HAYES
&
DAVID WHITEHEAD

SHERLOCK HOLMES
AND THE
QUEEN OF DIAMONDS

Complete and Unabridged

ULVERSCROFT
Leicester

First published in Great Britain in 2012 by
Robert Hale Limited
London

First Large Print Edition
published 2013
by arrangement with
Robert Hale Limited
London

The moral right of the authors has been asserted

Copyright © 2012 by Steve Hayes
and David Whitehead
All rights reserved

British Library CIP Data

Hayes, Steve.
  Sherlock Holmes and the Queen of Diamonds.
  1. Holmes, Sherlock (Fictitious character)- -Fiction.
  2. Watson, John H. (Fictitious character)- -Fiction.
  3. Detective and mystery stories.
  4. Large type books.
  I. Title II. Whitehead, David, *1958 –*
  813.5'4–dc23

  ISBN 978–1–4448–1388–3

Published by
F. A. Thorpe (Publishing)
Anstey, Leicestershire

Set by Words & Graphics Ltd.
Anstey, Leicestershire
Printed and bound in Great Britain by
T. J. International Ltd., Padstow, Cornwall

This book is printed on acid-free paper

For Chloe,
With Love from Steve
For Janet
With Love from Dave

Dyfed

Cl		Ac
	F	9630135546
S		In

Llyfrgell   Librar

1

Meeting in the Mist

London lay submerged in fog.

It drifted across swaybacked roofs and slanted chimneys, and brought with it a seeping, bone-deep chill as it all but smothered the feeble light thrown by the cast-iron streetlamps.

Huddled in the shadows thrown by one of the tall, white-stone buildings across from the dark, wooded acres of Green Park, Blackrat Lynch decided that he'd sooner be swilling grog down at the Poacher's Pocket, and toasting his frozen extremities around a blazing fire. But, appealing as that prospect was, it wouldn't put money in his pocket, and if there was one thing Blackrat was passionate about, it was money.

In the darkness behind him he heard the heavy, expectant breathing of his three companions — the shifty, pinch-faced little half-pint, Alfie Adams, the coffee-skinned mulatto, Olwenyo Wadlock, and quick-tempered Desmond O'Leary.

Like Blackrat, they had all been shaped by their times — born into poverty, the sons of drunkards and wastrels, reliant on the Overseer of the Poor to put food in their bellies and shirts on their backs. At first they'd been forced into larceny by a mixture of hunger and desperation, but it had been a more potent combination of simple greed and the lure of easy pickings that persuaded them to stay and hone their criminal skills in that murky underworld.

In the far distance Big Ben struck the hour. It was nine o'clock. Closer to hand, a stray dog started yapping. Alfie sniffed wetly and, as was his habit, sleeved his runny nose.

'I can't even *feel* me feet any more,' muttered O'Leary, clouds of vapour escaping from his mouth alongside the words. He tried to stamp some life back into them, until Blackrat hissed at him to keep the noise down.

''E's right, Blackrat,' whispered Alfie. 'We might as well give it up as a bad job. Ain't no one gonna come along 'ere tonight worth the robbin'.'

Blackrat made no immediate reply. They were right, of course, but he was loath to admit it. The pickings had grown slim in all their usual haunts, so he'd suggested they come up West, where they were more likely to encounter the well-off. Trouble was, the fog appeared to have kept everyone at home tonight.

'We'll give it five more minutes,' he decided stubbornly. 'If no one comes along by then, we'll call it a — '

He tensed suddenly, and, hearing the same thing that he'd heard, his companions followed suit. Mingled with the steady clip-clop of horses' hoofs coming hard and crisp against the mist-slick cobbles was the unmistakable sound of an approaching carriage.

'What did I tell you?' rasped Blackrat.

He pulled the stub of his hand-rolled cigarette from his lips and tossed it away. The orange tip quickly disappeared in the soot-speckled haze. Then he drew a short-bladed folding knife from his threadbare jacket, opened the blade and tightened his fingers expectantly around its black, screw-horn handle. Beside him, Alfie Adams sniffed again and produced a rusty cargo-hook. A tarnished knuckleduster glinted as Olwenyo Wadlock slid it on to his dark right fist, and Desmond O'Leary, always happy to fight when the odds were favourable, repeatedly slapped a billycock softly into the palm of his hand.

Blackrat, so named because of the discoloured buck teeth that showed grey against his heavy black beard, peered around the corner and grinned. The coach was a black brougham with red wheels, its yellow sidelights flanking the muffled driver on the high seat. Unless Blackrat missed his guess, their pickings were going to be rich here.

He gestured to his companions. Knowing from past experience what was expected of them, they immediately split up and vanished in a swirl of sulphurous fog.

The coach came closer along the centre of the street, pushing the yellow-red mist ahead of it. Closer it came . . . closer . . . until —

Alfie darted out in front of the vehicle, reached up and grabbed the bridle of one of the horses, yelling: 'Whoa there! Whoa! Whoa!'

At the same moment Wadlock and O'Leary attacked the carriage from either side. O'Leary put one size eleven hobnail on the wheel hub, launched himself up on to the seat, grabbed the startled driver by his muffler and jerked hard. The driver was pulled off the carriage and landed on the cobbles, dazed. O'Leary applied the brake, then jumped down beside him. Dragging the driver to his feet, he slammed him on the side of his head with the billycock. The driver dropped without a murmur.

Wadlock, meanwhile, had jerked open the

carriage door and started rummaging inside. The coach rocked furiously as a brief but inevitably one-sided struggle took place. At last the big mulatto withdrew his arm and Blackrat saw with approval that he had snared the only passenger — a woman.

A *handsome* one, at that.

As Wadlock pulled her out of the coach Blackrat ran his tongue across his scaly teeth. Beneath her red velvet cloak she appeared to be tall, elegant and opulently dressed. A tiara — diamonds set in silver and gold — nestled in the thick raven curls of her hair. At her throat was a matching necklace; and more diamonds sparkled from her earlobes and fingers.

The woman herself was perhaps thirty, with eyes the colour of very deep topaz above high, fine cheekbones. She had a short-bridged nose, full, scarlet lips and a firm, well-defined jaw. Her skin was pale and flawless, but anger now reddened her cheeks.

'Well, look what we got 'ere!' exclaimed Alfie.

The woman yanked her arm free of Wadlock's grip and was about to slap him when she heard Blackrat's slow, approaching tread on the cobbles. She whirled and narrowed her eyes at his short, thick silhouette.

'How dare you stop my coach!' she said.

Her American accent caused Blackrat to raise one shaggy eyebrow. Yanks — they rolled in money, they did. Still, there was no hint of panic in her voice, just fury.

'Beggin' yer pardon, Your 'Ighness,' he mocked. He stopped before her and executed an exaggerated bow. 'I really do 'ate to spoil your evenin'.' He sized her up, instinctively despising her for being so obviously wealthy. 'Been to the theatre, 'ave you, darlin'? Or some posh little soirée?'

O'Leary now joined the others, trapping the woman in a menacing half-circle. He had a face that was all angles and scars, the face of a merciless bareknuckle fighter, with soulless, pale-blue eyes and a scraggly, untrimmed moustache beneath his broken nose.

But still the woman showed more anger than fear.

'How dare you!' she repeated. 'Do you know who I am?'

'Well,' said Blackrat, studying her more carefully. 'You ain't ugly enough to be Queen Victoria.'

'I'm Elaina Montague,' the woman said, adding imperiously: 'Countess Elaina Montague. And unless you want the cat o' nine tails across your backs, you'll leave me be!'

'Oh, I don't think so, Your 'Ighness.'

Blackrat reached out quickly with his knife-hand and the blade sliced through the woven clasp of the countess's cloak. Wadlock grabbed the cloak and ripped it from her shoulders.

Blackrat grinned. He'd been right: tall, elegant and curvaceous. She wore an apple-green evening gown, the scooped neck revealing a promising swell of bosom, rising and falling rapidly now as she fought to control her rage. The fitted bodice tapered to a small waist, the skirt below it flaring from hips to ankles.

But his attention kept returning to the necklace, earrings and tiara. And that wasn't all the jewellery she wore. Her long fingers sparkled with rings; diamonds from South Africa, amethysts from Latin America.

Blackrat's mouth watered.

'I'll thank you for them trinkets, Your 'Ighness,' he said, moving closer.

And now Elaina *did* know fear, because a new, throatier quality had entered his voice, making her realize there were worse things than being robbed.

Sure enough, he confirmed it with his next statement.

'Then you an' me is gonna get to know each other a bit better in the back of your carriage, m'lady.'

His companions sniggered, Alfie sniffling and wiping his nose on his sleeve as he did so.

She looked at their leering faces and knew she was a bonus for them — a perk of the job. It wasn't enough that they had beaten and perhaps even killed Prescott, her coachman, or that they were going to steal her beloved jewels. They were also going to . . .

Knowing she could not allow such a thing to happen, she lashed out with her fist, heedless of the consequences. Her rings raked Blackrat's face. Blood ran from the deep scratches, reddening his unkempt beard. He staggered back, cursing her.

Immediately his men crowded her against the coach, grabbing and pinning her. She heard them swearing under their breath; felt their lust; smelled the rank odour of their unwashed bodies close to hers, and felt sick.

Blackrat put one hand to his ragged cheek, brought it away and inspected it in the meagre light. His palm glistened red. He looked at the countess and shook his head, as if to say she shouldn't have done that, and that things would go even harder for her now because of it.

Very deliberately he tucked his knife away and backhanded her.

She slammed back against the coach. Her cheek went numb. Enraged, she attacked him with flailing fists. For a moment Blackrat was surprised by her pluck and retreated. But then his mates joined in and, despite her desperate struggles, they soon pinned her against the coach.

'Get 'er inside,' hissed Blackrat, his voice now hoarse with lust.

The others had just started to obey when a voice behind them said quietly: 'Hold it, gents!'

Blackrat spun around to see who had spoken. On the pavement a short distance away stood a tall, lean man in a wide-brimmed, flat-topped Stetson hat. He wore an unbuttoned brown sack coat and matching pants, a black waistcoat over a cotton shirt, with a narrow blue necktie. His expression was neither grim nor angry, yet there was something inexpressibly menacing about him.

Blackrat immediately reached for his knife, subconsciously bulking himself up to present a more intimidating front.

'An' who the bleedin' hell are you?' he demanded.

The newcomer faced him square on. 'Someone you don't want to mix it up with,' came the softly spoken reply.

A cool grin made Blackrat's beard stir slowly. 'You got two choices, mate,' he said. 'You can keep walkin' and pretend you never saw nuffink, or you can poke your nose into our business an' get your arse kicked inside out.'

Though the odds were against him the stranger seemed untroubled by the threat. He didn't smile, but something in his eyes hinted that he was more amused than frightened by Blackrat and his henchmen.

'Well,' Blackrat demanded belligerently. 'What's it to be?'

The stranger considered for a moment. A man worth looking at twice, he had a tanned, intelligent, well-sculpted face and deep-set, light-blue eyes. His nose was thin and straight, his mouth narrow with tight white lips. Below, a faint, reddish-blond goatee beard couldn't quite hide his cleft chin.

Eventually he said: 'I advise you to let the lady go.'

Blackrat grinned at his companions: 'Well, bugger me sideways. I do believe we've caught ourselves two birds with one stone tonight.' And then to the stranger: 'Time to teach you to mind your own business, mate.'

He and his henchmen turned their backs on the countess and advanced menacingly toward the newcomer, but he showed no fear as they closed in, only a kind of reckless, joyful anticipation.

'I'm sorry you have to see this, ma'am,' he said, politely tipping his hat to the countess.

'But they don't leave me any choice.'

Even as he finished speaking he quickly crossed his arms so that each hand reached under the opposite armpit. They reappeared a split second later, each filled with an ivory-handled Colt .45. As he aimed the guns at the robbers, he thumbed the hammers back so that they were ready to fire.

Cli-cli-click!

At the sound, Blackrat and his pals froze.

' 'Ere, 'ere, let's not be 'asty, guv!' Blackrat said hurriedly. 'I mean, we didn't know this 'ere lady was a friend of yours or we never would've bothered 'er. Right, lads?'

'Never, mate,' Alfie sniffed.

The stranger regarded them mockingly. 'I gave you fair warnin'.'

'That's right,' agreed Blackrat, bobbing his head eagerly. 'An' we was wrong to ignore it. But we won't never make the same mistake again, mate. We'll go straight from now on, God's truth we will.'

The tall American let him babble on for a few moments, then said: 'You fellers have put me in an awkward spot. See, I don't want to have to shoot you, 'cause it'll mean breaking my word to someone, but at the same time I can't let you get away with assaultin' this lady . . . ' He paused, as if trying to find a solution.

'P-Please, mister,' Blackrat begged, sounding dangerously close to tears. 'Don't shoot us. We won't never do nothin' like this again. 'Onest.'

Still the stranger offered no mercy. There was a cold hardness in his eyes that made it clear he had killed before, and more than once.

But rescue came from an unexpected source.

'It's all right,' said Elaina. 'I'm sure they . . . they've learned their lesson. You can let them go.'

The stranger showed no sign of hearing her.

'Please,' Elaina added. 'I don't want anyone killed on my behalf.'

At that the stranger seemed to relax and some of the grimness left his eyes.

'In that case,' he told the footpads, 'it looks like tonight's your lucky night, boys. So *git*.'

'Bleedin' good idea, that,' said Blackrat.

' 'Fact, it was just what we was about to do,' agreed Alfie.

Wadlock and O'Leary both nodded.

The stranger watched them scurry off into the fog. Only when their hurried footsteps had faded altogether did the guns in his hands vanish back into the folds of his coat.

He crossed to the countess and retrieved

her cloak. 'Here, let me, ma'am . . . ' He shook it out and then reached around her to drape it gently across her strong shoulders. The action was gentlemanly and chivalrous, but also very close to an embrace.

The countess looked into his face and saw a man of perhaps her own age. She started to thank him. Before she could do so, he turned and was gone, swallowed up in the fog.

For a moment Elaina was disappointed. Then she realized that he had only gone around the coach to check on her driver.

She followed him, heels clicking loudly in the fog-muffled street, and found him kneeling beside the coachman, who was now sitting up, gingerly feeling his head.

'You all right, mister?'

Prescott forced himself over on to his hands and knees and reached for his fallen hat. 'Yes, sir . . . I'll . . . I'll be fine in a jiffy, sir.'

Elaina knelt beside them, said: 'Thank you, Mr, uh . . . '

'Howard, ma'am,' the stranger said. 'Thomas Howard. From Missoura.'

Elaina extended her right hand. 'I've never been so glad to see a fellow American,' she replied. 'I'm Countess Elaina Montague — and I'm beholden.'

To her disappointment he merely shook

her hand instead of pressing it to his narrow lips. But it was the very wildness in him, that sense of raw and untamed sensuality that excited and intrigued her in equal measure.

'If you hadn't come along when you did — ' she began.

'Best not to dwell on *ifs*, ma'am. Important thing is, I *did* come along.'

'Yes, and thank God you did or . . . ' She stopped as she realized she was embarrassing him with her gratitude.

Turning, he helped the coachman regain his feet. Prescott looked pale and shaken and there was a nasty swelling on his temple, but, notwithstanding he announced that he would live. 'I'm sorry, m'lady,' he said sincerely. 'It happened so quickly, they took me by surprise.'

'No harm done, Prescott,' Elaina said. She moved to her carriage before turning to the stranger. 'Can we drop you anywhere, Mr Howard?'

'That's OK, ma'am. I got things to do.'

Again she felt disappointed. 'You'd be doing me a favour if you'd accompany me home,' she said shamelessly. 'I'm a little shaky after what's happened.'

He gave her a curious look, for she certainly hadn't struck him as the shaky type. 'In that case, ma'am, it'd be my pleasure.'

He helped her into the coach and then got in after her. Prescott closed the door and climbed back on to the driver's seat. A moment later they heard him cluck and the horses leaned into the harness. With a gentle jolt they started moving forward again through the murky night.

'Have you been in London long, Mr Howard?'

He was peering out at the foggy streets. His profile, caught whenever a passing streetlamp touched it, showed that he was clearly preoccupied. 'No, ma'am. Just a few days.'

'And what brings you to England — business or pleasure?'

When he continued to stare out of the window, she said: 'I'm sorry, I didn't mean to pry.'

He turned to her. 'It's me who should apologize, ma'am. I never was much for talkin', but since you asked . . . I'm looking for someone. My kid brother, Hank. He came here a while back and . . . well, no one's heard from him since. He's a wild colt, and I promised Ma I'd try to find him.'

Elaina's face showed genuine concern. 'Why, that's terrible. Is the Yard helping you look for him?'

'The 'Yard'?'

'Scotland Yard — the police.'

15

'Nope. I ain't involved the police yet, ma'am.'

'Well, you'll have to, sooner or later. This is a big city, Mr Howard, and not at all like back home. The population of London alone is about five million. You won't have much luck looking for one man all by yourself.'

'Thanks. I'll, uh, be sure'n talk to 'em.'

Even as she heard the lack of conviction in his tone, an idea hit her. 'Wait a minute!' she said. 'You might not *need* the police! I may be able to help you myself!'

'Excuse me, ma'am?'

'I know a man — a detective. He's a curious duck, but he knows his trade. I'll ask *him* to help you.'

'I wouldn't want to put you to any trouble, ma'am,'

'It's no trouble, Mr Howard. In fact, I've been wondering how I could repay you for rescuing me, and this is the perfect way.'

'But it's late, and — '

'Hush,' she said. 'I've made up my mind. And when you get to know me better, you'll know that once I do that, there's no changing it.' Impulsively she leaned forward and called out of the window: 'Prescott — 221B Baker Street, if you please!'

16

2

An Open Book

Dr John Watson leaned back in his chair beside the dying fire and closed his eyes. He had once been a strongly built man, a little above average height, with a thick neck, a square face and a small moustache. But now, even after a long recuperation, he was still just a shadow of his former athletic self.

He'd gone to Afghanistan as an assistant surgeon with the Army Medical Department and returned a casualty of the battle of Maiwand, where he had been wounded once in the shoulder and once in the leg. His recovery had been slow, and indeed was still ongoing, but upon his return to England he had had the good fortune to fall in with Sherlock Holmes, the world's first — and, so far as he knew — only consulting detective. This had ensured that he rarely had time to brood over his injuries.

At the moment, however, the persistent throb of his leg wound could no longer be ignored. It seemed to Watson that even the most subtle change in the weather could aggravate it, and he'd had enough of its persistent dull ache for one evening.

He was just reflecting upon how curious it was that the less serious of his two wounds should be the one to cause him so much lasting discomfort when the doorbell rang. He looked at the clock. It was late for visitors, especially on a damp and foggy night like this. But perhaps the visitors were here to see their landlady, Martha Hudson.

A few moments later, there came a discreet rapping at the door, and Watson sighed wearily. Rising, he grasped his cane and limped across to see who it was, the prospect of a hot toddy and a rest in a warm bed vanishing by the second.

Mrs Hudson stood outside, tiny hands clasped before her, her round face dominated by wide blue eyes, her manner hushed and apologetic. 'I'm sorry to bother you so late, Doctor, but you have visitors. Should I tell them to go away and call again in the morning?'

He was tempted to say yes. It had been a long day and he was exhausted. But before he could reach a decision a figure emerged from the shadows at the head of the stairs and, with a rustle of silks and satins, pushed past the landlady, saying: 'You'll do no such thing,

Mrs Hudson! I'm sure Dr Watson will be only too happy to receive us.'

Without giving Mrs Hudson a chance to argue, Countess Elaina Montague swept into the large, airy sitting room, gesturing that her companion should follow her. After a moment's hesitation he did. Watson saw a man of about his own height but slimmer and more muscular, who was clearly ill at ease, turning a black, flat-topped Stetson between his fingers.

Watson squared his shoulders, dismissed Mrs Hudson and then offered the man his hand. The fellow had a strong, firm grip.

'Mr Howard,' said Elaina, 'meet Dr John Watson. Dr Watson — my newfound friend, Mr Thomas Howard.'

Howard nodded a vague acknowledgement, but his attention had already been taken by the eccentric nature of the room. In one corner stood a stool and a chemical-burned workbench. On the other side of the rear window someone had marked out the letters 'V.R.' — presumably for *Victoria Regina* — in what looked like bullet-holes. A sheaf of letters was affixed to the mantelpiece by a jack-knife, and nearby was a human skull and a magnifying glass. On top of the bookshelves in the opposite corner lay a selection of weapons: a serpentine *kris* from the East, an axe — even a horseshoe and a wax head depicting a stern-faced man with hollow cheeks.

Watson indicated for them both to be seated on the sofa. Though he had no great love for Elaina, he would never be anything less than civil toward her. 'I fear you may have had a wasted journey, Countess. Holmes is out at the moment.'

'Off trying to solve yet another riddle?' she asked playfully.

'Actually, he's gone to the theatre.'

'The theatre?'

'Well, the music hall, to be precise. What you would call *vaudeville* in America, Mr Howard. The varieties.'

'I had no idea Holmes had any interest in popular entertainment,' said Elaina.

'Nor did I,' confessed Watson. 'But he's visited practically every music hall in London over the past few weeks. It's as if he cannot get enough of — '

Before he could finish the sentence they heard the street door close and then the steady tread of someone ascending the seventeen steps to the first floor. 'I believe you may be in luck after all,' said Watson, and a few moments later the door opened and Sherlock Holmes stood within its frame.

Although he was dressed formally in a

black cutaway coat and matching trousers, he looked more like a vague, ethereal spirit than a man. He was very tall — more than six feet — and lean almost to the point of emaciation. Oiled black hair swept back from a high, pale forehead. Two sharp grey eyes flanked a long, hawk nose. His cheeks were hollow, his mouth thin, jaw square. It was the face of a man who studied all things with equal fervour, a man obsessed with the accumulation of knowledge, no matter how seemingly obscure. It was the face of the man depicted by the wax bust on the bookshelf.

As he stared at Elaina it was difficult to decipher his expression. Holmes had devoted his life to the art of deduction and had little time for the niceties of polite society. Often, Watson thought of him as more machine than man, one who thrived upon challenge and despised inaction. And yet, as Watson observed him now, he saw something all too human in his friend — a wholly uncharacteristic desire within him; a desire for the countess.

Holmes crossed the room, took Elaina's hand and held it to his thin lips a moment longer than necessary. 'Countess,' he said softly. 'It has been too long since last our paths crossed.'

She smiled, pleased by his flattery. 'They

wouldn't be crossing now if it hadn't been for this brave gentleman, who saved my life.'

'Your life?' asked Watson.

For the first time Holmes regarded Howard.

'Yes,' Elaina said. 'Singlehandedly, Mr Howard here drove off a gang of cut-throats who were about to rob and kill me.'

'Then I am indebted to you, sir,' said Holmes, shaking hands with him.

Howard looked embarrassed. 'She's makin' way too much of it, Mr Holmes. All I did was 'persuade' a few weasels that their skins were more important than the lady's jewels.'

'Don't believe him, Holmes,' Elaina said. 'He's being far too modest.'

'One of the traits of a true gentleman,' said Holmes, hooking his top hat on the coat rack and smoothing back his hair. 'Even one who hails from Missouri, lives in the saddle and yet has the good taste to wear custom-tailored suits and hand-tooled boots.'

Howard stared at Holmes, not sure whether he was being complimented or ridiculed.

Elaina said: 'Don't be shocked, Mr Howard. Knowing everything about a person after just meeting them is one of Holmes's party tricks. Tell him how you do it, Holmes.'

Holmes gestured for them to sit on the sofa

and then slumped into the fireside chair facing the 'V. R.' symbol. 'Actually, Mr Howard, determining who you are and where you're from was quite easy. Not only is the cut of your suit clearly American, but your Midwestern accent holds the unmistakable trait of Missouri folk, wherein all the vowels are pronounced as if they were '*a*' — 'Missoura' for instance, instead of 'Missouri'. So — I put your place of birth and residence as Missouri, though I have yet to train my ear to the subtle inflections which would enable me to pinpoint a particular area.'

'I'll save you the trouble,' Howard said, his tone chilly. 'I'm from Kearney.'

Elaina suddenly sat up, exclaiming: 'Really? I'm from Kansas City! No wonder fate threw us together. We're neighbours!' She glanced at Holmes. 'I'm sorry. Please go on guessing.'

'It is not guesswork, Countess,' he corrected. 'It is elementary deduction. To the sufficiently observant, everyone is an open book. Some are more able to 'read' them than others.' He treated Howard to another searching scrutiny. By his expression it was obvious that the man from Missouri disliked being the object of such attention.

'I perceive, sir, that you are an outdoorsman,' Holmes continued at last, 'and that it is uncommonly hot where you come from. You ride a great deal and, like so many of your countrymen, you carry guns, though not at your waist, as is customary in the colonies, but since you came to England, in shoulder-holsters.'

'Isn't he marvellous?' Elaina exclaimed.

'Marvellous ain't the word,' growled Howard. 'OK — how'd you do it?'

'I just told you — simple observation. Your complexion tells me that you spend much of your time outdoors. The squint lines around your eyes indicate that you are constantly in the sun, which in turn tells me that you come from a hot climate. The high heels on your boots make walking long distances uncomfortable, but of course are perfectly suited for riding stirrups.'

'And the shoulder-holsters?'

'Your suit, Mr Howard. Though custom-tailored, the tightness across your chest suggests that you had it made *before* you acquired your shoulder-holsters.' Holmes paused momentarily, then said: 'Perhaps you acquired them in the belief that the purchasing and carrying of firearms in Great Britain was illegal? It isn't, you know. One only has to go to the nearest post office and buy a licence.'

'You're just a *world* of information, ain't you?'

'No, sir — *you* are. Your surname, for example, which derives from the Old Norse *Howard* or *Herward*, tells me that you have Welsh ancestry. The careful way in which you took your seat just now informs me that you have suffered a chest wound or similar injury in the past, perhaps during your late War of the Secession? It healed several years ago, but can still be aggravated by damp weather, such as that of tonight. I note that you have also spent your life veering from wealth to poverty and back again.'

Howard threw a dark look at Elaina, as if blaming her for bringing him here and subjecting him to what must surely be some kind of sorcery.

'And this, uh, *book*,' he asked belligerently. 'Does it say what I do for a living?'

'No, but your hands do. When we shook a moment ago, the calluses told me that you are neither a banker nor an accountant.'

'Then what am I?'

'Gentleman farmer? Cattleman, perhaps?'

Howard eyed him narrowly. 'You know somethin', mister? You got a strange way of sayin' a thing. You make it sound halfway between a compliment and an insult, and I ain't sure I like it.'

'I meant no offense,' Holmes replied innocently.

25

Watson, having already sensed the friction building between the two men, moved quickly to defuse the situation. 'May I offer you a drink, Mr Howard?'

Howard shook his head. 'I don't think so. Reckon I'll be movin' along.'

'Oh, no! We're here now,' said Elaina. 'At least let's tell Holmes the nature of your problem.'

'He don't need to know what — '

'Nonsense.' Elaina turned to Holmes: 'Mr Howard's brother has gone missing and I was hoping you'd help find him.'

'That may not be possible,' said Holmes. 'You are familiar with the recent spate of jewellery thefts, of course?'

'Of course. I know a number of the victims personally. In fact, I'm holding a little gathering for several of them tomorrow afternoon. I was hoping it would cheer everyone up.'

'I am presently engaged upon the case,' Holmes continued. 'Thus, my time is limited. However, it can do no harm to hear your story, Mr Howard. You may speak freely before Dr Watson, and of course in complete confidence. Your brother came to England and vanished. What brought him here to begin with?'

Howard's discomfort increased visibly. 'I'm

not sure this is such a good idea, you bein'
busy elsewhere and all. Maybe I'll just — '

'Oh, do tell him,' Elaina urged. 'If anyone
can help, Holmes can.'

'What brought your brother here to begin
with?' Holmes repeated.

'What takes a man anywhere?' Howard
replied vaguely. 'Opportunity. The promise of
a better life.'

'And he did not feel he could find that
better life in Missouri?'

'No.'

'Was there any particular reason he should
feel that way?'

'Uh-uh.'

'So he came to England.'

Howard nodded.

'He didn't go looking for opportunity in a
neighbouring state or territory?'

'Nope.'

'Then I suggest he is a fearless and perhaps
ambitious man. How old is he, Mr Howard?'

'About twenty or so.'

'Did you have an address for him here?'

'No. He just said he'd write when . . . ' He
made a sudden impatient gesture, adding:
'Look, I got no idea where he is or how to
find him. And for all your powers of
observation I doubt you'll do much better,
Mr Holmes, so let's just leave it at that, OK?'

Holmes considered him for a moment, then smiled and nodded. 'As you wish. May I suggest, however, that you file details of your, ah, brother with Scotland Yard, and perhaps Mr William Booth's East London Christian Mission, in Shoreditch.'

'I'll do that,' said Howard, rising. 'Sorry we wasted your time.'

'My time is never wasted, sir,' Holmes said, also rising.

Elaina frowned at Howard. 'Hold on. Let's not be so hasty. It's been quite an evening. Maybe we should discuss this again tomorrow, when we're all a bit fresher. Holmes, please . . . consider yourself invited to my tea party tomorrow. You too, Watson. Mr Howard, you'll be there, won't you?'

'Well, I — '

'Good,' she said, cutting him off. 'That's settled, then.'

At the door Howard regarded Holmes coolly. 'One last thing. I can see how you came to your conclusions. But that business about me veering from wealth to poverty an' back again . . . that's got me stumped.'

'It is quite simple, sir,' said Holmes. 'When in funds you had the suit you now wear tailor-made for you. When you lost the third of its four jacket buttons you were so poor that you had to replace it with an odd one

— and judging from the amateur quality of the stitching, you sewed it on yourself.'

'And comin' back into 'funds'?'

'Simplicity itself, Mr Howard,' Holmes said with a rare smile. 'Had you not come into money again, you would not have been able to buy your passage to England.'

3

The Poacher's Pocket

In the Poacher's Pocket, a notorious public house just a stone's throw from the Pool of London, Blackrat Lynch and his three pals sat at a knife-scarred corner table and commiserated over mugs of ale. The scratches on Blackrat's craggy face had already excited much raillery from the regulars — 'What's'a matter, Blackrat? The old woman givin' you grief again?' — and he was in a foul mood.

Around them, by contrast, the pub's other patrons were thoroughly enjoying themselves. They crowded around tables to play shuffle-board or put 'n' take, sat on rough-hewn benches and leaned against the bar, while mingled with the constant chatter were great howls of laughter. Occasionally there were cheers and someone broke into slurred song. The smoky air stank of fried fish, cheese and pickles.

'We should'a rushed 'im,' said Alfie, wiping his runny nose on his sleeve.

'Aye,' O'Leary agreed. 'Y'know, the more I

t'ink about it, the more I t'ink he was bluffin'.'

Blackrat took the hand-rolled cigarette from his mouth and said: 'Well, think what you like. But I knows we did the right thing, givin' 'im the benefit of the doubt. Still,' he grumbled, 'it do leave a rotten taste in the mouth.' He shook his head and added through gritted teeth: 'What I wouldn't have given to slip a blade 'tween that bastard's ribs.'

At just that moment a shadow fell across him, and a soft voice said: 'Buy you a drink, pal?'

The American accent sent a stab of alarm through Blackrat. He twisted hurriedly in his chair, expecting to see the man who'd held them at gunpoint. Instead he saw two strangers in belted mackinaws buttoned to the throat — a pock-faced man, who'd asked the question, and a younger, darker-haired man standing just behind his left shoulder.

Blackrat relaxed, but thought: *Another bleedin' American. This city's full of 'em tonight.* 'An' who're you?' he asked.

'Someone who's heard about what happened to you earlier tonight and wants to hear more.'

Blackrat frowned, surprised that the news had travelled so fast. But then he remembered that he and his lads had been

31

bemoaning their fate all the way from Green Park to Cable Street and the Poacher's Pocket.

Still, who were these two Yanks who'd come out of nowhere to hear them tell the story one more time? And why should they be so interested?

'Jack,' the speaker said over his shoulder, 'go buy a round for our new friends here.'

The dark-haired one, Jack, nodded and went to the bar.

The pock-faced man helped himself to a chair, turned it around and straddled it so that he could cross his arms on its back. He was big and brawny, perhaps thirty, with unkempt fair hair above a creased forehead, a heavy brow, deep-set hazel eyes and a long nose. 'I'm Micajah Liggett,' he said.

'That's nice for you,' Blackrat said disparagingly.

The pock-faced man smiled, not a pretty sight, and taking no offence, said: 'My friends call me Cage. That feller with me, that's my brother Jack. And you're Blackrat Lynch, right? Right — so now we know each other. So let's hear your story again.'

Blackrat was happy enough to tell it, but didn't much care for the way this Liggett character made it sound like an order. 'Why?' he demanded. 'What's your interest in it?

Mate of yours, is 'e, this other Yank?'

'Not if he's the man I think he is.'

Jack returned and set a tray on the table. Blackrat and his men helped themselves to tall glasses of black, bitter ale. Jack sat beside his brother, though it was hard to think of them as such. Where Liggett was fair Jack was dark. Where Liggett was tall and powerful, Jack was short and slight. Where Liggett wore a thick handlebar moustache, Jack was clean-shaven. The only thing they seemed to have in common was the same shifty, hazel eyes.

'I'm waitin',' Cage Liggett said.

Blackrat shrugged and told his version of the story. He made the man with the pistols seem like a bully, while he and his pals came off like victims. At the end of it, Liggett said: 'What did he look like, this stranger?'

Blackrat peered at him. 'It strikes me, mate, that you're expectin' an awful lot for one lousy pint of ale. If this man's so important to you, you oughta be 'appy to *pay* for 'is description.'

Liggett's eyes hooded. 'Don't go wakin' up the wrong passenger, Blackrat,' he warned softly. 'Let's just keep this nice an' friendly.'

But Blackrat was in no mood to keep things nice and friendly. Though they hadn't said as much, he felt that he'd lost standing with his companions tonight and needed to reassert himself. So he said: 'I got a better idea. You make it worth our while to talk, or you sling your bleedin' 'ook while you still can.'

Liggett sighed regretfully. 'Sorry you feel that way, friend. 'Cause now I got to teach you a lesson.'

'You an' whose army?' snarled Blackrat.

Whipping out his knife, he lunged at the big American, but Liggett moved faster, flinging the ale in his tankard into Blackrat's face. Momentarily blinded, Blackrat pawed at his eyes and then stumbled backward, falling over the table.

Seizing the advantage, Liggett knocked the knife from the Londoner's hand. Then, pulling Blackrat's cap down over his eyes, Liggett belted him on the side of the head. The blow sent Blackrat sprawling on the floor.

Instantly, all the other customers turned to watch the fight.

Brawls were common in the Poacher's Pocket and friendships were few. When two men quarrelled over something the matter was invariably settled with knuckles or blades. Those around them seldom interfered. But as Liggett kicked his chair away and closed in to finish his opponent off, Blackrat's companions jumped up, intending to attack the American.

Jack quickly drew a Colt .45 and cocked the hammer back. 'Stay out of it, you buzzards,' he warned them. 'Just sit down and keep your hands on the table, where I can see 'em.'

Alfie, O'Leary and Wadlock grudgingly obeyed.

The rest of the patrons immediately cleared a space for the combatants and Liggett danced forward, determined not to disappoint them. He waited until Blackrat got back to his hands and knees and then kicked him in the ribs. The impact lifted Blackrat off the floor. He rolled over, grunting. But he recovered faster than Liggett expected, grabbed the American's boot by heel and toe and twisted. Forced off balance, Liggett stumbled back against the table, sending table and chairs flying across the sawdusted floorboards.

Blackrat jumped up, fists swinging wildly. Liggett blocked his blows and then jabbed Blackrat several times in the face. Blackrat staggered back, blood streaming from his nose. Liggett charged in, hammering him with punches, forcing Blackrat to retreat still further.

He stumbled against a table. He grabbed a bottle from it, smashed the bottom off then brandished the jagged neck in Liggett's face.

Liggett fell back, watching him warily. The onlookers abruptly fell silent. Liggett tore his mackinaw off and wrapped it around his right hand and forearm.

Blackrat lunged at him before he was finished. At once the crowd roared. Liggett quickly snaked the jacket out so that it wrapped itself around Blackrat's knife-arm. He yanked back on the coat, pulling Blackrat forward, into a bone-shattering left hook. Blackrat's legs went wobbly and he collapsed on the floor. Liggett kicked the broken bottle away, then dropped to his knees beside Blackrat and started punching him repeatedly in the face. He kept up the onslaught, blow after vicious blow, until Blackrat's face was so much raw meat.

Helpless, Blackrat was soon beaten unconscious. The onlookers, accustomed to seeing Blackrat the victor, again fell silent. No one had ever seen any man destroy his opponent so thoroughly, and a grim hush settled inside the pub.

At last Liggett stopped punching and just stood over Blackrat, his powerful shoulders heaving as he sucked in air. Then, retrieving his jacket, he turned to Alfie, O'Leary and Wadlock and said: 'Gentlemen . . . I give you your . . . fearless leader.'

Alfie looked down at Blackrat, his weasly

face a portrait of disappointment. First the man with the guns, and now *this*. 'Forget it,' he said, sniffling and wiping his nose. ''E ain't our leader no more.'

'That go for all of you?' Liggett asked the others.

The trio exchanged looks. Then, as one, they nodded.

'Then take the trash out before it stinks up the place, boys. And get back in here soon as you can.' He turned to his brother. 'Jack — set 'em up again. We got some talkin' to do, and we're gonna start with a description of the man with the guns.'

'You got it, guv'nor,' Alfie said.

'An' I'll hear the straight of it,' Liggett warned. He spotted the fallen knife and picked it up, admiring its unusual screw-horn handle before closing it up and slipping it into his pocket. 'No lies, no exaggerations. You guys play fair with me and I'll play fair with you. Got that?'

Three heads nodded eagerly.

4

The Crippled Acrobat

Holmes, who normally slept till noon or beyond, was woken early the following morning by a persistent rapping at his bedroom door. When he answered it, he found Watson standing there holding a yellow telegram envelope.

'This has just arrived. I didn't know if it might be important.'

Holmes took the envelope, tore it open and quickly scanned the contents. A moment later he vanished back into his room, calling through the now-closed door: 'Get your coat, Watson, and ask Mrs Hudson to summon a cab at once! We're off to Surbiton.'

'Surbiton?'

Holmes's door opened again and he looked out. 'Yes. That telegram was from our old friend Rosier of the Yard. Our jewel thief has struck again, this time at the home of Lady Bingham!'

While Holmes saw to his ablutions Watson collected his coat, pulled his cane from the rack by the door and hurried downstairs. As always, Mrs Hudson was busily engaged in her domestic chores, so he went outside, dug his cab-whistle from his pocket and gave a single shrill blast. A hansom soon drew up and Watson was just about to ask the driver to wait when Holmes, now washed, shaved and dressed, brushed past him. 'Witton Abbey, Surbiton,' he told the driver. 'And there's a bonus in it for you if you can get us there in half the time it normally takes!'

The driver saw this as both a challenge and an opportunity to earn some extra money, so the journey was almost as reckless as it was fleet. As Watson was jostled back and forth inside the cab, he chided Holmes for endangering their lives. 'After all,' he grumbled, 'is there really any call for such speed? The crime has already been committed. We're too late to do anything now but investigate such clues as may have been left behind.'

'That is precisely why we *must* hurry, Watson. Rosier is an admirable chap, quite one of the brightest men Scotland Yard has to offer, but even *he* runs the risk of contaminating or quite possibly eliminating altogether what little evidence there may be. If we cannot prevent such damage, the least we may do is limit it.'

The journey took them through the fashionable sprawl of Mayfair, past the gasworks and breweries of industrialized Wandsworth and at last to the historic market town of Kingston-upon-Thames. It had rained during the night but now the sun started breaking through the louring clouds, and everything looked as fresh and clean as a picture postcard.

From Kingston-upon-Thames it was a relatively short hop to the picturesque lanes and meadows of Surbiton, and presently they came within sight of Witton Abbey, as the Bingham estate was known.

It was a large Gothic-style house built from big white-stone blocks, with long, rectangular windows running along the ground floor and smaller sash windows along the second. As the hansom turned off the lane on to the gravel drive they saw a black carriage that doubled as transport for police or mobile cells in which to remove criminals, and a separate hansom.

Barely waiting for their cab to stop, Holmes sprang from the vehicle and hurried to the front door. Telling the cabby to wait, Watson limped up the steps to the front door just as it was opened by a soberly attired butler.

Before Holmes could introduce himself an authoritative voice behind the butler said: 'It's all right, Draper. Come in, Mr Holmes. I knew you'd want to be in on this.'

The speaker was Inspector Maurice Rosier, a tall, tow-headed man dressed in a black herringbone suit and a striped school tie. Holmes held him in some regard, for unlike many of his ilk he had courage, tenacity and no small intelligence. He came forward, moving in a peculiar, predatory manner that was unique to him, and shook hands. 'The bugger's really outdone himself this time,' he confided. 'Stolen a necklace valued at five thousand pounds, and I'm at a loss as to explain exactly how he did it.'

'You have your men out searching the grounds?' asked Holmes.

'Of course, sir.'

'Then ask them to stop at once. Nothing further is to be moved, examined or inspected until I say so.'

Rosier raised his eyebrows. 'Very good, sir. I'll pass the word.'

He disappeared for a few moments, then came back and led them into a large sitting room, where Lady Bingham, a tall, thin woman who wore her grey hair in ringlets, sat on a sofa, dabbing at her eyes.

'Mr Sherlock Holmes and Dr Watson, my lady,' he announced. 'Mr Holmes has followed the case from the first and kindly offered his services in order to bring the thief to justice.'

Lady Bingham stood up and allowed each of them to take her fingertips and nod respectfully. 'It's terrible,' she said. 'That necklace has been in my family for two generations. It is made up of three strings of stones of various sizes and shapes, all of which are black — jet, onyx and jasper. I have worn it ever since my husband died, for that is its primary purpose, to denote mourning. It is irreplaceable.' Her voice cracked a little, but with effort she managed to retain her composure.

'Then between us, Lady Bingham, Inspector Rosier and I will endeavour to return it to you as quickly as possible,' replied Holmes. 'If I might ask you a few questions, my lady?'

'Of course.'

'When did you first notice the necklace was missing?'

'Last night. My husband died some seven months ago and I have worn it as a sign of my great sorrow ever since. I did not go out yesterday, so there was no need to wear it. However, when I retired last night I noticed that the box I kept it in had been moved.'

'Moved?' Holmes repeated.

'I like things to be orderly, Mr Holmes,' Lady Bingham explained. 'A place for everything and everything in its place. So naturally I noticed at once that it had been moved, if only fractionally, and when I checked inside the box — '

' — the necklace was gone?'

'Yes.'

'And that was the only piece of jewellery that was missing?'

'Yes.'

'No attempt was made to take anything else of value?'

'No. Everything else was just as I had left it.'

'Neither you nor any of your servants happened to see the thief or scare him off?'

'Certainly not.'

'May I ask what time you retired last night?'

'Half past nine, exactly,' Lady Bingham said. 'I know because the grandfather clock in the main hall was striking the hour as I climbed the stairs.'

'And the house was occupied during all that time?'

'Of course.'

'You have questioned the staff, Rosier?'

'Naturally,' the inspector said. 'The kitchen, where the back door is situated, is overlooked by the servants' hall, which was occupied all evening by the wine steward, the butler, the housekeeper and the lady's maid. No one could have entered or left by that way without being seen. Neither were there any callers.'

'And nothing out of the ordinary occurred, that might have served as a distraction?'

'Nothing.'

'And your staff, Lady Bingham — you trust them?'

'Implicitly. They have been with me for years, Mr Holmes, and their loyalty is beyond question.'

'Quite so.' Holmes paused. 'May I have your permission to examine your bedroom, my lady?'

'If you must,' she said reluctantly. 'If it helps you to find my necklace.'

'It may well do.' Holmes smiled. 'Will you lead the way, Inspector?'

They bowed courteously and then Rosier took them up a wide flight of stairs to Lady Bingham's bedroom, which was at the back of the house. It was a large, airy room that overlooked landscaped grounds, and everything was indeed in its place, as her ladyship had assured them. Holmes went first to the dressing-table, where he opened the lid of the engraved sterling-silver jewellery box and examined its contents. Lady Bingham's jewellery was stored neatly in two tiers of blue velvet-lined compartments. Only one of them was empty. He brought the box to his face and appeared to sniff the contents. Accustomed to Holmes's unorthodox and often seemingly eccentric methods as Watson was, even he had to frown.

Holmes set the box back on the dressing-table, then went over to the first of the two windows. Each was of the sash type and secured by a two-piece brass fastener. First he inspected the fastener, then unlatched it, threw up the window, leaned out to the waist with his thin-fingered hands on the sill and surveyed the terrace and gardens far below. There was a folly, an orangery, neatly maintained trees and shrubs all the way down to the river at the bottom of the field. A fine mist obscured the tops of the trees.

Holmes studied the sill and then twisted around so that he could examine the outside of the frame. A moment later he closed the window, and repeated the procedure with the second window. At last he nodded to himself.

Next he took off his jacket and handed it to Watson, then climbed unhesitatingly out into the sill.

Watson immediately panicked. 'I say, old man, hang on. What on earth are you — ?'

Holmes ignored him. Holding on to the window frame, he straightened to his full height on the outside of the glass, seemingly oblivious to the precarious position in which he had placed himself. He reached up, the expression on his lean face intense. Watson watched with concern, uncomfortably aware that one slip or a stray gust of wind and Holmes would plunge to the flagstones below.

But at last Holmes calmly withdrew his right hand, sniffed at his fingers and allowed himself the briefest smile. He then climbed back into the room and collected his jacket from Watson, who shook his head disapprovingly.

'Holmes,' he said, concerned, 'without a doubt there are times when you completely confound me.'

Holmes beamed, as if he'd been given a compliment. 'If I may quote from Sir Walter Scott,' he countered, 'Faint heart never won fair lady.' Now — I believe we have discovered everything this room has to offer.' Leaving his companions to exchange a puzzled glance, he marched out of the room.

They followed him downstairs and through the kitchen to the back door. Outside, under the curious gaze of the assembled police constables, Holmes turned to face the rear wall of the mansion and then hurried to the far end, where a galvanized iron drainpipe climbed towards a hopper and a line of guttering above. He inspected the drainpipe with great care, seemed to find something that piqued his interest and examined it more closely with the help of a magnifying glass. After taking a penknife and an envelope from his pocket he carefully scratched at a small black mark that was just below eye level. Watson and Rosier watched as the mark came off the drainpipe in a series of soft black flakes.

'What's that?' asked the inspector.

'I expect that closer examination will reveal it to be high-grain leather.'

'Then it's a clue?'

'Rather a confirmation,' said Holmes.

The evidence collected, he placed the envelope in an inside pocket and then set off across the grass toward a row of hedges in the distance. Intrigued, Watson and Rosier hurried after him. By the time they caught up, Holmes had reached the bank of the river and was creeping slowly through a cluster of bushes. Next he walked down toward the riverbank, where he bent double in order to study the dewy grass. A few moments later he straightened up, cocked his head at the ground as if making some sort of calculation. Then he peered into the murky water before dropping to his stomach, so that his face was mere inches from the surface.

They watched him move along the bank in this fashion for a few minutes, until at last he sat up again, once more removed his jacket, rolled up his sleeves and took a tape measure from his waistcoat pocket. With the tape held between the thumbs and forefingers of both hands, he plunged his arms up to the elbows into the cold water. Shortly, he brought them out again, studied the dripping tape measure closely, then nodded.

Eventually he regained his feet and dried himself off with a handkerchief. 'Most instructive,' he remarked.

'What have you discovered?' asked Rosier.

'Almost everything, Inspector.'

'*What?*'

'There were two thieves,' said Holmes. 'They arrived by rowing boat. From the indentations left in the mud as they came ashore I should say the clinker-built construction points to a simple skiff. They made the vessel fast just there — ' he pointed ' — by tying a hemp rope to yonder bush. One of them was a largish man, perhaps fifteen stone in weight. The other was much smaller, barely seven stone, who walked with a limp. A *limp*, Watson,' he added, as if it should mean something.

'How can you possibly know that?' Rosier asked.

'By measuring the depth to which the bow sank into the mud when they climbed out, I calculate that their combined weight was somewhere in the region of twenty to twenty-two stone. Their footprints, as they came ashore, indicate that one was considerably heavier than the other — the depth of his footprints is approximately twice as deep as those of his companion. As for the limp, look here. Can you see where the stride is uneven? At no time does the stride of the left foot ever overtake that of the right. It merely draws level with it.'

Watson and the inspector peered closer and saw that Holmes was right. Holmes, meanwhile, needing no mere mortal confirmation of his brilliance, turned back to the riverbank. 'The heavier of the two fellows stayed here,' he continued, 'with the boat, while the smaller one went to the house alone. He climbed the drainpipe and — '

'Just a moment, Mr Holmes,' Rosier said. 'Are you telling me in all seriousness that a smallish man with a bad leg shinned up that drainpipe, slick as it was from last night's fog?'

'It is beyond dispute, Inspector. Unless I am very badly mistaken — which I assure you I am not — the sample of high-grain leather I took from the pipe will match that found in any soft ballet shoe. May I continue?'

'Please do.'

'Having climbed the drainpipe, the thief took hold of the guttering visible there just below the base of the slate overhang and, using the grooves or recesses between the cement blocks as toeholds, made his way along to Lady Bingham's window. There he crouched on the sill and used a penknife — certainly nothing with a wider blade — to force the catch. If you take a closer look at the brass fastener on the second window you will find a series of hairline scratches made by the cutting edge of the knife as it was slipped between the top and bottom halves of the window. Once in the room he stole the item he was after; then, using the knife to reset the latch, left the same way.'

Watson and Rosier were studying the house. 'I don't mean to call your judgement into question, Mr Holmes,' said the inspector, 'but . . . well, it would be a rare or hopelessly greedy cove who'd attempt something as dangerous as that.'

'I am inclined more towards the former than the latter,' said Holmes, slipping on his jacket. 'At any rate, that is how it was done. Examine the drainpipe carefully and you will find several superficial scratches approximately five feet from the base. These, I believe, were made by the buckles of leather gloves used specifically for the purpose of gripping. Once my examination of the high-grain leather is complete, I expect to find it a close if not identical match to that used in the manufacture of ballet shoes. Finally, if you examine the lip of the aforementioned guttering, you will find evidence of magnesium carbonate — simple climbing chalk — used to keep our thief's palms dry during both ascent and descent. It has a peculiar smell reminiscent of cloves. It may be that cloves have been added to the mixture because of the calming properties they are said to possess.'

He was silent a moment. Then he repeated, almost to himself: 'A limp! This really has been a most constructive morning's work.'

'But does it help us catch our man?'

'Frankly, Inspector, 'our man', as you put it, is largely unimportant. He does not steal for himself. He steals to order. And that makes him but a mere link in the chain.' He pinned the tall inspector with an earnest look. 'Please tell her ladyship that we have made great progress here today, and that I will not rest until she and her sentimental necklace are reunited. Come, Watson, we have work to do. I cannot *believe* I have been so blind, nor wasted so much time because of that blindness!'

He was gone almost before either of them realized it.

Holmes seemed energized by his efforts and Watson had a struggle to keep up with him as he hurried back round the house to their waiting cab. 'Where to now, then, Holmes?' he asked.

Holmes's glance implied that the answer should have been obvious. 'Tavistock Street, of course, and the offices of *The Era*, my dear fellow.'

Watson frowned. 'That theatrical rag?'

'The actor's *bible*,' Holmes corrected.

'And what do you expect to find there?'

'Our thief, naturally.'

'I'm sorry, Holmes, but I'm afraid I still don't follow.'

'Then allow me to explain. So far we have had four robberies. In each case, a lady's bedroom has been the target, and one specific item of jewellery has been stolen. In the case of Lady Darlington-White's rare teardrop earrings, our thief climbed a tree and gained access to the roof of the property by means of an overhanging branch. From there he was able to attach a rope to the nearest chimney stack, climb down from above and in that way gain entry to her ladyship's bedroom. In the case of Baroness Alcott's gold diamond pendant I deduce that he climbed the ivy covering the front elevation and entered by means of a window that had been left open for ventilation. For the robbery of Countess Broughton's pearl bracelet he took a more obvious route, using a ladder that had been left for the night by some roofers who were repairing the flashings on the property at the time. What does this imply to you?'

'That our man is ingenious,' Watson said. 'And has nerves of steel and no fear of heights.'

'And what person could perform such feats and live to tell the tale?'

Watson considered the question and then shrugged, stumped.

'I put it to you, my dear Watson, that the person we are after is an aerialist — someone used to heights and climbing, possessed of great balance and nerve. And that is the person I have been trying to find all these weeks.'

At last something made sense to Watson. 'Your sudden interest in the music hall . . . ?' he began.

'Of course, Watson. Have you any idea how many music halls we have in the metropolis? Close to eighty, the over-whelming majority of them wretched fleapits employing a seemingly endless procession of third-rate comedians, jugglers, singers and fire-eaters, and I have sat through every tedious act just to watch the aerialists and acrobats in the hopes of spotting my man. Of course, I realize now that I have been wasting my time, for while I remain convinced that our thief possesses that particular skill, he clearly no longer performs it.'

'Because of the limp?'

'Precisely. So now we shift the focus of our enquiry. We are looking for a performer who had an accident and damaged his left leg. It has clearly not impaired his abilities, but has certainly ruined his career, for what enjoyment can there be for the audience when one of the performers has to limp on to the stage?'

'So he is the man we have to find in order to discover the real brains behind the crimes, eh?'

'It is possible. However, there is another reason. I feel some compassion for this man, who is as honest as the day is long. I would not care to see him arrested and thrown into prison. That would only add insult to injury.'

Watson looked perplexed. 'You've lost me again, Holmes. How, pray, can a thief be as honest as the day is long?'

'Think about it. In every case he has been

charged with stealing one specific item of jewellery, and that is precisely what he has done. A less honest man would almost certainly have taken a little something extra for himself. Not so this one.'

'And for that you believe he deserves a second chance?'

'"Judge not lest ye be judged",' said Holmes. '*Matthew*, seven: one.' As they climbed back into the hansom he checked his pocket watch. 'We still have a full day ahead of us. First we'll fortify ourselves at one of the coffee shops in Covent Garden, and then we'll spend an hour or so going through *The Era's* archives. And let us not forget we've been invited for tea at Countess Elaina's this afternoon.'

'As if I could forget,' Watson replied morosely.

Holmes gave a rare chuckle. 'Cheer up, old friend. As far as such social events go, I rather fancy this particular one will be somewhat livelier than most.'

5

Tea-Party

Elaina Montague checked the spelter clock for the umpteenth time and then turned her attention back to the bow window that overlooked the gravel drive fronting the house. It was just after one o'clock and all but one of her guests had already arrived and was now seated in the elegantly-furnished library, sipping tea, eating daintily cut, finger-sized sandwiches and discussing the topics of the day. Among them was a photographic journalist from the *Illustrated London News*. He was there to describe the gathering for the society pages, and presently was taking notes and hanging on every word, especially if it dealt with gossip.

After a dismal start the day had finally started to brighten. But Elaina's heart still felt heavy. The previous night she had dropped Thomas Howard at his lodgings, a rather mean boarding house in Houndsditch, where he had thanked her for her kindness in taking him to see Sherlock Holmes and apologized if his behaviour had seemed rude or ungrateful.

'Reckon I prefer to do this thing my own way, ma'am,' he'd concluded. 'And to be straight with you, I found that Holmes feller a hard man to like.'

'Please,' she said. 'If anyone should apologize, it should be me for dragging you along when clearly your heart wasn't in it. It's just that I wanted to help. I *still* want to help. And I still think Holmes is the man to find your brother. You may not like him, but he really is a remarkable person.'

'Maybe so. I just wouldn't want to share a jug with him, ma'am.'

'Then we'll say no more about it. And we'll have no more of *mister* and *ma'am*, either. I am Elaina, but I'd prefer you to call me Ellie. And unless you have any objections, I shall call you Thomas.'

'If it pleases you, ma' — I mean, Ellie.'

'It does. And I have another suggestion. This ... hostelry of yours ... is a rather seedy place; far too seedy for a gentleman like yourself. Why not come and stay at Montague Hall, as my guest? You can stay as long as you like and you'll be free to keep your own hours.'

It was the last thing he'd been expecting, and it showed in his face. 'That's kind of you, but — '

'Come, now, Thomas. Surely you wouldn't prefer to stay where you are?'

'Ma'am, it's a mighty generous offer. But I couldn't impose. Besides, I don't reckon your husband would cotton much to you bringin' home a stray hound like me.'

'My husband is dead,' she said flatly.

'I'm sorry.'

'Don't be. It's been eighteen months since he died. On top of that it was a stupid accident — one he could have easily avoided.'

Undecided, he studied her through the fog. He was where he needed to be right now, on the fringes of the East End. And yet the prospect of enjoying a little comfort and female company while he was here was tempting; especially a female as sensually attractive as the countess. Then he made a decision and Elaina felt a shiver run through her when she saw the bold interest that entered his expression. 'OK,' he said finally, 'I'll accept your generous offer.'

'It's settled, then,' she said, brightening. 'Pack your bags and I'll have Prescott pick you up tomorrow, say about noon.'

'I'll be there,' he assured her.

But now, almost twelve hours later as she again looked at the clock, she wondered if Thomas Howard had had second thoughts. Surely he and Prescott should have been here by now. What possibly could have happened to detain them?

'Uh, excuse me, my lady.'

She turned to see the photographer from the *Illustrated London News* hovering at her shoulder. 'Yes, Mr Prendergast?'

'I wonder if I might ask a few questions?'

'Uh . . . not just now, if you please. I'm still awaiting the arrival of a very important guest.'

'As you wish.'

The party was a chore, as these events always were for her. Though she had deliberately set out to become part of the elite London society, she'd never quite fitted into it; neither had her guests ever gone out of their way to make her feel anything but an outsider. Of course, they'd played the game and pretended to make her feel welcome, particularly when her husband had been alive. They'd had no wish to offend the Earl, who was richer than all of them combined. But after his death certain lubricious rumours had started circulating; and while they kept up the thin pretence of civility, she had seen it in their eyes — contempt, mistrust, envy and a powerful desire to be scandalized by her.

She had obliged them, she supposed. She had attempted to break every rule of etiquette just to make their jaws drop and their eyes bug, and she had succeeded beyond her wildest hopes. When she rode, she rode like a man, in pants and boots, astride the horse, not side saddle. She smoked, she drank, and on occasion she swore. And because she had inherited her husband's wealth, they had no choice but to accept scandalous behaviour in silence because they knew she could have her lawyer, Sir Ashley Danvers-Cole, use virtually any means to break them if they didn't.

Today, however, they had other matters to concern them. Rumour had spread that Lady Bingham had been robbed the night before, and presently that was all her guests seemed to want to talk about. When Elaina confessed that she too had almost been robbed the previous night, Lady Spence declared that she just didn't know what the world was coming to.

'I think we're too soft on the criminal classes,' she went on. 'In fact, I think the Home Secretary should seriously consider the reintroduction of transportation to the colonies.'

This met with enthusiastic agreement. 'Bring back stocks, pillories and public whippings, I say,' declared Victor Landon, a plump and prominent civil engineer. 'And make hard labour harder still. Punishment

— the more severe the better — is the only language the criminal classes seem to understand.'

'Hear, hear!'

Elaina finally excused herself and went through the large house to the front door, where the guests' coaches were parked along a gravel drive that led toward the walls and gates which separated Montague Hall from the rest of Richmond. The Hall was a 500-year old mansion built on the grassy banks of the Thames, and by any stretch of the imagination it was magnificent. There was a square central wing, or pavilion, three stories high and built in the Italian style, with a square belvedere tower at either end. She opened the door, hoping to see her brougham approaching, but still there was no sign of it and her smile died almost as quickly as it was born.

'Is everything all right, my lady?'

She was just about to turn and answer the butler's query when she spotted movement beyond the gates at the far end of the drive. A moment later the black-and-red brougham came into view, and she stifled a giggle. She might have known it! There was the brougham . . . and there was Thomas Howard, riding shotgun on the high seat, beside Prescott!

'Yes, Fordham,' she said to the butler. 'Thank you.'

She went out on to the steps to greet the coach. It seemed to take an eternity before Prescott wheeled it to a halt in front of her. Howard, dressed as he had been the previous night, climbed down, looked at the house and whistled softly.

'Sure we got the right address, Prescott?' he called back to the driver. And then, as Elaina laughed: 'Well, one thing's for sure — we ain't in Kansas.'

Again Elaina laughed and this time offered him her hand. 'You're late, Thomas. What kept you?'

He shrugged. 'Sunup I decided to take that Holmes feller's advice and go visit that Christian mission he talked about. They couldn't help me, but while I was in that part of the city I took another look around the docks an' kind of lost track of time. Your man was waitin' for me when I got back.'

'Well, you're here now,' she said, 'and that's all that matters. Fordham, please take Mr Howard's bag up to the guest room Sally prepared this morning, if you please.'

'Yes, my lady.'

As Elaina impulsively took his arm, Howard caught something in her smile that told him he wouldn't be spending too much time alone in that room — or maybe that was just wishful thinking on his part.

'Now, come and meet my guests,' she said, leading him inside. 'I know they're dying to meet *you*.'

As they entered the enormous, high-ceilinged foyer Howard stopped and stared about him. Its white walls were covered in portraits and frescoes, and on the marble floors stood Romanesque plinths supporting exquisite busts. To him it looked more like a museum than a place where folks lived.

'What's wrong?' Elaina asked.

He grinned. 'Just wonderin' how a girl from Kansas ends up with all this?'

'She needed a lot of luck,' Elaina said. ''Course, having a genuine real-live earl staying at her father's hotel didn't hurt none.'

'I didn't know there *were* any genuine real-live earls in Kansas.'

'There aren't. Not anymore.'

'What was a British earl doin' there in the first place?'

'Hunting buffalo. We never would've met, but one of his entourage accidently shot himself in the leg and the nearest doctor was in Kansas City, a few blocks from our hotel — '

' — and that gave *you* the chance to meet him?'

'And for *him* to meet *me*,' Elaina said, smiling.

'Why do I have a feelin' that it wasn't a fair fight?'

She laughed, all of her earlier misgivings now melted away. 'Straighten your tie, Thomas Howard. You're about to make acquaintance with the cream of British high society, and I want you to look your best.'

He glanced around self-consciously as she led him into the library. The oak-panelled room was a storehouse of Queen Anne furniture, shelves lined with priceless tomes and French windows overlooking terraced lawns that sloped gently down toward the river.

Elaina's gentlemen guests rose to their feet and shook Howard's hand. The ladies stayed put and allowed him to dip his head respectfully and kiss their fingertips. Elaina realized he was making an effort to behave himself and play the game, just as she did, and she smiled appreciatively. But he soon tired of being the centre of attention. He felt more like an object of curiosity than anything else, as much a thing to be studied by all these lords and ladies as by Sherlock Holmes the night before.

One of the servants gave him a cup of coffee. But as he was asked one cliché question after another, his mood darkened. At last he got bored and stared through the French windows at the manicured lawns and the line of trees beyond, wishing he could be out there in the fresh air, away from this sickly stench of cologne and perfume and obscene wealth.

An overweight, bejewelled woman Elaina introduced as Lady — hell, he'd already forgotten her name — asked him what he did in Missouri.

'He's a cattleman, Elspeth,' Elaina answered smoothly.

Lady Chatfield's pencilled eyebrows rose a notch. 'Oh, are you one of those rustlers the books talk about?'

'Elspeth!' said one of the women beside her. 'Shame on you. You've actually *read* those dreadful whatever-they're-calleds?'

'*Penny dreadfuls* is the term, my dear,' put in her bewhiskered husband.

'I haven't actually *read* them, Daphne,' Elspeth said hurriedly. 'But I confess, I did find one in the servants' quarters the other day and gave it a quick peek. Quite stimulating' — catching her own husband's look of disapproval, she added — 'in a revolting sort of way, of course.'

'In answer to your question, Elspeth,' said Elaina, 'no, Mr Howard is *not* a rustler.'

'Stealin' other folks' cattle is a necktie offense, ma'am,' he explained.

'Necktie offense'?'

'Hangin', ma'am.' And in case he hadn't made himself clear enough, he mimed hanging, bugging his eyes, poking out his tongue, making gurgling noises and pretending to twist the end of an invisible rope.

It had the desired effect. Lady Chatfield and company might be happy to suggest all manner of dire punishments for the criminal classes, but they recoiled at the grotesque sight one of those punishments might look like.

'O-Oh, dear me, do rustlers steal?' asked Elspeth. 'I am so dreadfully sorry, Mr Howard. I had no idea — '

'Forget it, ma'am. I know you ain't on the prod.'

'On the what?'

'Tryin' to rile me. Twist my tail. Get my goat?'

'Oh-h, no, of course not. I'd never even *touch* a goat's tail, let alone twist it.'

'If you'll excuse us,' Elaina put in, 'we simply *must* mingle.'

As they moved on, she said through her fixed smile: 'Thank God I don't have to see these pompous idiots too often. I'd die of boredom.'

Howard scowled. 'What I can't figure out is how folks can speak the same language and not understand each other.' He pulled up suddenly and nodded toward a man with a heavy moustache, who was busily working over a sketch patch.

'Who's that feller?'

'He's a sketch artist from the *Illustrated London News*. He's recording the event for the society pages.'

'He keeps lookin' at me.'

'Maybe he's sketching *you*.'

'He better not,' he growled.

She cocked her head at him, surprised by his reaction. 'Don't tell me you're like the Indians,' she said, trying to make light of it. 'They believe that if someone takes your photograph or draws your picture they take your soul along with it.'

'It ain't that,' he murmured, suddenly disentangling himself from her. 'Listen, I'm gonna tell that there feller to quit drawin' me.'

She frowned, alarmed by the change that had come over him. 'You don't *really* mind, do you?' she asked. 'I mean, we *have* ascertained that you're not a rustler.'

But for the moment at least his sense of humour appeared to have deserted him. Without another word he strode across to the sketch artist, yanked the pad out of the startled man's hands, turned it around and glanced at the portrait he'd been working on. His mouth thinned when he saw that it was an excellent likeness of himself.

'I'll take this,' he said softly, and before the artist could do more than open and close his mouth a few times in surprise, he ripped the portrait from the pad, crumpled it up in one fist and shoved it into a jacket pocket.

'But . . . but . . . ' was all the artist seemed able to manage.

'Don't you go drawin' me again, mister,' warned Howard. 'I don't cotton to it.'

They stared at each other for a moment, the artist's hazel eyes both puzzled and fearful. There was something about Howard that thoroughly intimidated him, and he could only sigh with relief when a voice behind the man suddenly called: 'I say there, Mr Howard!'

Howard glanced around. 'What is it?' he asked testily.

If he sensed Howard's dark mood, Victor Landon certainly didn't show it. He said jovially: 'They tell me you're from America, sir — Missouri, of all places! I spent some time there last year, on business. Saw some of the locals perform the most marvellous tricks with a lariat. How are you with a rope, sir?'

Howard shrugged, deciding to settle with the sketch artist before the party ended. 'I reckon I can handle one,' he allowed. 'But I didn't bring mine with me. Didn't figure I'd need it.'

'Surely you can find a length of rope, Elaina?' Lady Chatfield said.

When everyone else chimed in, begging Howard to perform some tricks, Elaina sent Fordham in search of a length of rope. He returned shortly with a coiled washing line. 'I'm afraid this is the best I could do, my lady.'

Howard took it, got the feel and weight of it, and said: 'Best do this outside.'

Caught up in the excitement, Elaina clapped her hands and called: 'Outside, everybody! Mr Howard is going to entertain us.'

She opened the French windows and led Howard outside. Everyone followed them out on to a wide paved terrace overlooking the formal gardens. Immaculate lawns and rose gardens were surrounded by stands of spring-blooming ash, birch, beech and wych-elm, all of them dwarfed by a single massive oak that occupied the centre of the main lawn. In the far distance, hawthorn, blackthorn and holly sheltered against the old red-brick wall that enclosed the grounds.

The terrace itself was enclosed by a low wall, upon the coping stones of which sat a series of small terracotta flowerpots, each one holding amaryllis, gardenia, phlox or other spring flowers. As he walked, Howard quickly fashioned a small eyelet in the rope. Through this he threaded enough rope to make a loop of about five feet in diameter.

When his audience had gathered around, he arranged the loop on the ground beside him. Silence fell as he began to spin the loop, which slowly rose off the ground for a few inches and began to revolve ever faster. Everyone applauded, but this wasn't the trick — it was merely what came *before* the trick.

A moment later he hopped into the spinning loop and began switching the free end from left hand to right and back again, around and around him, at incredible speed. The loop rose ever higher, first to his knees, then his waist, then his shoulders and finally high overhead. The loop whirled up around him like a well-trained snake, causing the onlookers to gasp with admiration.

Under his control, the loop began to descend past his head and shoulders, then below his waist to his calves. Now, spinning it one-handed, he stepped out of the loop, then back in. He repeated the procedure several times, so that he appeared almost to be skipping. Once again his audience burst into applause.

Enjoying himself, he continued to perform. He allowed about three feet of the rope to dangle from his left hand. His audience watched expectantly. Then he turned his wrist suddenly and the end of the rope flew backwards over his arm, forming a loop as it did so. At the same moment he jerked the eyelet up and caught the loop. He shook the rope off his arm and let it fall, and there, tied into the rope, was a perfect pretzel shape.

Once again there was a burst of applause. Once again Howard repeated the procedure, allowing the last three feet of the rope to dangle from his left hand. Turning his wrist sharply he caught the end in the eyelet, but this time when he shook it out it described a near-perfect figure eight.

'Bravo!'

'Well done, sir!'

He shook the rope out again and began to spin the loop vertically beside him. Women cocked their heads in curiosity. Men scratched thoughtfully at their sidewhiskers. Then Howard hopped sideways, right through the loop, only to hop back again just seconds later. He repeated the trick twice more, and then brought the loop up so that it was spinning directly over his head.

Again the guests fell quiet. The only sound now was the whoosh the rope made as it sliced through the air, leaving a vacuum in its wake. At last he cast the loop and a gasp went up as it fell neatly over Elaina's head, pinning her arms to her sides. While everyone around them clapped, Howard slowly began to draw her to him, hand over hand. Elaina, acknowledging the cheers, went towards him, laughing like a young girl.

She thought he would stop pulling when she was almost to him, but he didn't. He kept drawing her closer until they were standing face to face, almost touching. There was something so intimate in the moment that the applause and cheering faltered a little and suddenly turned uncomfortable.

'Better let me go before they get the wrong impression,' she whispered through a smile.

'Or the *right* one,' he said with a sly wink.

With one movement he removed the loop and then turned and bowed. The good humour immediately returned.

'More . . . more . . . do some more!'

Encouraged by the reception, Howard threw the rope aside, unbuttoned his jacket and suddenly pulled out his ivory-handled six-guns.

An uneasy silence descended upon the terrace. Even Elaina's grin began to look strained.

'All of you,' said Howard, 'keep well back.'

Everyone quickly obeyed.

Howard began to spin the guns by their trigger guards. They flashed and winked as they spun first one way, then the other. Then he started flipping them over his shoulders and under his arms, and soon the watchers started to clap and cheer appreciatively. The guns seemed to be alive as he flat-spun them, then made them cross in mid-air. He caught them by their barrels, spun them again and then, almost faster than anyone could see, they were snug back in their holsters.

Acknowledging the appreciation of his audience with a casual wave, he set himself with legs spread and knees slightly bent. Then, almost faster than the eye could follow, a gun appeared in his right hand and a shot boomed out in the chilly afternoon. One of the flowerpots resting on the low terrace wall exploded, spraying terracotta and dirt every-where. Howard's audience, who'd never seen the like before, went wild. As they clapped and cheered he fired again, three quick shots, and one after another the adjacent flowerpots exploded in spectacular fashion.

The gun was back in leather before anyone saw it happen. Immediately, he drew his other gun and three more shots echoed through the afternoon. The heads of three flowers burst apart.

'I say, good show, Howard!' cried Landon.

Howard grinned, feeling that he had at last gained the acceptance of these idle rich and, caught up in the moment, he aimed at the head of a fourth flower.

But before he could fire there was another gunshot and the flower disintegrated. Howard spun around, eyes hooding like those of a cornered wolf.

He saw Holmes and Watson standing in front of the French windows. They had clearly just arrived . . . and Holmes was holding a smoking revolver in his right hand.

6

Jealousy

For one long moment no one moved. Then Elaina broke the spell, hurrying back to the house to greet the newcomers. 'Holmes! I was wondering when you were going to show up,' she exclaimed.

As she approached, Holmes deftly spun the gun by its trigger guard and handed it back to Watson, butt first. 'Here, Watson — your service revolver returned with thanks.'

Watson accepted it with a look of disapproval. But Holmes only had eyes for Elaina as he pressed her hand to his lips. At last his keen eyes found those of Howard and he nodded with respect.

'My compliments, sir. You are quite the marksman.'

'You're no greenhorn yourself,' Howard said. Gun still in his hand, he slowly approached Holmes. 'Accordin' to my brother, you English don't care to go around packin' iron. And yet here you are, loaded for bear.'

'We only go armed when the situation

demands it,' said Watson.

'Like a tea party, you mean?'

'Of course not. But when Holmes here tells me to carry my revolver, I carry it. Had he told me that his only intention was to use it for show, however, I would have thought twice. Firearms should be treated with more respect.'

Howard indicated the revolver. 'You mind?'

Before Watson could argue, Howard took the gun and examined it with interest. 'Never seen one of these before.'

'It's a Webley mark two,' Watson said stiffly.

Howard hefted its weight, felt the way the grips fitted his palm, then whirled and fired it. On the other side of the terrace the head of another flower vanished in a small but dramatic explosion of petals.

Holmes gave a faintly mocking smile. 'Do *you* mind, Mr Howard?'

Howard hesitated, then drew one of his Colts, spun it by its trigger guard and handed it to Holmes. As he took it, Holmes said: 'Ah. Mr Colt's famed Peacemaker.'

'You know your weapons, I'll give you that.'

Holmes sidestepped, snapped his arm out straight and fired. Flame tore from the barrel and yet another flower burst apart.

Again their audience clapped. But Elaina, sensing the growing tension between the two men, quickly stepped between them. 'Before you destroy *all* my flowers, gentlemen, may we call this little competition a draw?'

'A diplomatic solution,' said Holmes, 'but not one that I could accept. I have no doubt that Mr Howard could shoot rings around me, if he so chose.'

'There you go again,' said Howard, bristling. 'Makin' a compliment sound more like you're spittin' in my face.'

Forcing a smile, Elaina turned to her guests. 'Show's over, ladies and gentlemen, and since it seems to be clouding up I suggest we go back inside and enjoy some more refreshments.'

★ ★ ★

For the remainder of the afternoon Howard gave Holmes and Watson a wide berth. But he surreptitiously kept an eye on them to make sure they didn't get a chance to surprise him again.

Watson, meanwhile, was troubled by Holmes's attitude toward Howard. He had known Holmes long enough to recognize just how out of character it was, and decided to await the right moment to question it. The moment came as they were standing in a corner of the library sipping their tea and observing the other guests. 'You know, Holmes,' he said quietly, 'sometimes I just do not understand you.'

Holmes lifted one eyebrow. 'I fear that few people do,' he replied. 'But I see from your expression that you have something specific over which you would like to take me to task?'

'I do. This Howard fellow. Ever since you first set eyes on him, you seem to have gone out of your way to goad him . . . even belittle him. Doesn't the poor man already have enough problems of his own without having to endure your sarcasm and veiled insults as well? Good God, man, how would you feel if your younger brother went missing overseas?'

'Ah, yes,' said Holmes, unfazed by Watson's chiding, 'his missing brother. I had quite forgotten about him.'

'You never forget *anything*, so don't try to deceive me with that. I must say, though, you seem to have taken an instant dislike to that man and for the life of me I can't understand why — ' Watson broke off abruptly as it hit him, then said: 'Good Lord, you're not *jealous* of him, are you?'

'Don't be ridiculous.'

'No, no, you are. I can tell.'

'And why, pray, would I be jealous of him?'

'I suggest that it has to do with whatever

relationship he appears to be cultivating with the countess.' Watson shook his head, both amazed and amused. 'Sherlock Holmes, the man who once told me that even the best of women weren't to be trusted!'

Holmes eyed him sharply. 'Might I suggest that you take out your handkerchief and wipe that look of disapproval from your face?'

'Very funny,' Watson said grimly. 'I don't need your keen analytical mind to work out what's going on here. But have a care, Holmes. That woman has a reputation — a most unenviable one. As your friend I feel I should advise you to have nothing to do with her.'

'Listen to yourself, Watson. If anyone is exhibiting signs of jealousy here, it's *you*.'

'That's a damnable thing to say.'

'Damnable, perhaps. Accurate — certainly.'

Watson drew himself up and his moustache seemed to bristle. 'I didn't realize it was a crime to care what becomes of one's best friend,' he grumbled. 'Good heavens, Holmes, you know as well as I do that she pushed her husband down the stairs.'

'Until you have solid evidence to corroborate that statement, it remains little more than idle gossip, Watson, pure speculation — and that is something I never respond to.'

'Then respond to this. What about her

promiscuity? Good God, Holmes, the infernal woman has been . . . well, *intimate* . . . with more men than England has colonies.'

'My friend, you know that my interest in the countess is purely professional.'

'I always thought so,' Watson said. 'Now, I'm not so sure.' He set his cup and saucer down, seemingly hurt by Holmes's rebuttal. 'Perhaps I should just leave you to it. If you like I'll return to the offices of *The Era* and continue searching their archives for your crippled acrobat.'

'I should be most upset if you do,' replied Holmes.

'Why?'

'Because things promise to get altogether more interesting here before much longer.'

★　★　★

Presently late afternoon darkness began to settle over the serene Richmond countryside. The pleasant chirruping of birds was replaced by the insidious whine of flying insects. Lights began to glow in the windows of the surrounding houses and taverns. Streetlights were lit, illuminating passing hansoms. Nightlife began.

But as far as Watson was concerned, things at Montague Hall remained exactly as they were — tedious. At long last, however, Elaina's guests started making their farewells and taking their leave.

'We must be leaving too, Countess,' said Watson with no small relief. 'But it has been a most pleasant afternoon.'

'I'm glad you enjoyed it, Doctor,' Elaina said. 'But if you don't mind my saying so, you're a lousy liar.'

As Watson cleared his throat in embarrassment, Holmes said: 'You are as direct as you are beautiful, Countess. Unfortunately for Watson, he is as uncomfortable with the one attribute as he is at home with the other. Would you care to share a cab with us, Mr Howard?'

Howard glanced at Elaina before answering: 'No, thanks.'

'Mr Howard is staying on as my guest,' she explained.

Holmes eyed her for a long, hard moment before saying: 'I see.'

'Actually, you don't,' she said. 'Neither you nor Dr Watson.' She guided them toward the door, adding: 'But I can tell you this. Offering a fellow countryman a place to stay is a small price to pay for his saving my life last night.'

Holmes's mouth tightened into a thin line. 'Of course,' he said flatly. Then with a polite nod: 'Good evening, Countess.'

Outside, as soon as the door closed, Watson wasted no time heading for their waiting hansom. 'At last!' he said with feeling. Then, when his friend didn't respond: 'I was beginning to get worried. You're normally the last man to wear out your welcome, Holmes, but couldn't you see they were *aching* for us to leave?'

'Of course I could. Why else do you think I refused to make a move?'

Watson rolled his eyes. 'Holmes, you've always been insufferable, but I have the dreadful feeling you have just become more so!' He buttoned his jacket. 'Now, shall we get a move on? Pastries are all very well, but Mrs Hudson is serving roast mutton tonight!'

Holmes shrugged and slowed his pace. 'By all means go along, old friend.'

'What about you?'

'I promised you that things were about to become interesting. Don't you want to find out just *how* interesting?'

Without waiting for a response, Holmes turned and started walking back toward the house.

7

En Garde!

The Earl of Montague's armoury was housed at the rear of the mansion. It was a large, musty, high-ceilinged room with lead-paned windows, suits of armour, Montague pennants and weapons of all shapes and sizes mounted on the cold, grey stone walls. Four centuries of weaponry were collected here — and all of it had tasted blood on some near or distant battlefield.

Howard, who'd shown interest in the place as soon as Elaina had mentioned it, now studied a pair of overcoat pistols from the time of George III before moving on to a selection of long-barrelled sporting guns and even an old Brown Bess musket from his own country. And the blades — there were swords from Britain and France, sabres from Russia and Austria-Hungary, dirks, cutlasses, spadroons . . .

Howard whistled. 'I reckon a feller could fight off a whole army with all this,' he said, his voice echoing faintly off the cool, rough stone.

A few feet away Elaina watched him with a motherly smile, for he was like a child in a toyshop. 'According to Rupert, that's exactly what the Montagues *did*, on many occasions,' she replied. 'Apparently there were Montagues at the battles of Hastings and Stamford Bridge, at Saratoga, Trafalgar, New Orleans . . . oh, just about everywhere, to hear the way Rupert told it — and of course, they *always* acquitted themselves with tremendous courage.'

'Of *course*,' he replied, and laughed.

Howard helped himself to a narrow-bladed fencing sabre, which had been hanging from hooks on the facing wall. He gave it a couple of practice swipes. They confirmed his initial impression — that it was the product of a remarkable craftsman.

'What kind of man was your husband, Ellie? Don't take this the wrong way, but you make him sound like a blowhard.'

'He wasn't,' she replied after a moment's thought. 'Not really. Decent just about sums him up. Though he could certainly be a windbag at times, like most of this country's ruling class. They all think God's an Englishman, you know.'

'Do they also all give left-handed compliments?'

She smiled. 'No, that's just Holmes being

. . . well, Holmes. Don't take it personally, Thomas.'

'It's a little too late for that.'

He looked at her suddenly, saw a hunger in her eyes that was the match of his own, and impulsively went to her. He wrapped his free arm around her shoulders, pulled her close and kissed her, full and hard on the mouth. She kissed him back with equal fervour until . . .

There was a discreet rapping at the door.

For reasons neither of them could have explained, they sprang apart like guilty lovers. Blaming it on the heated passion she felt, Elaina called out in a steady voice: 'Come.'

The door opened to reveal Fordham. 'I'm sorry to disturb you, my lady, but Mr Holmes has just returned and asks to see you.'

Howard swore under his breath, but before she could react, Holmes — who had ignored the request to wait in the library and instead had followed the butler through the house to the armoury — entered the room with Watson tagging along behind. Fordham discreetly withdrew, closing the door after him.

The moment was especially awkward for Watson. He could see that they had interrupted what appeared to be an intimate moment, and he looked as if he would rather be anywhere but here.

Not so Holmes. He looked from Elaina to Howard, a thin smile tilting his mouth. 'Forgive the intrusion,' he said, clearly not meaning a word of it. 'But just as we were leaving Watson reminded me that we had not enquired after your, uh, brother, Mr Howard.'

'My brother?' Howard said blankly.

'You remember,' said Holmes sarcastically. 'The missing one. It occurred to me that if you would sooner conduct your search for him by yourself, the very least I could do is suggest a few avenues that may make the job somewhat less arduous for you.'

Howard relaxed. 'Don't bother. I'll find him in my own good time.'

'As you wish,' Holmes said. For the first time he appeared to notice the fencing sabre in Howard's grip. 'Do you favour the steel, Mr Howard?'

'You mean, can I *use* one? Sure. After the War, I — ' He caught himself then, and said: 'How about you?'

'Like all men of education, I deplore violence.'

Howard's jaw muscles flexed. 'That a yes or a no?'

'If you are suggesting a duel, Mr Howard — I would rather not.'

Howard had been suggesting no such

thing, of course, but now that the idea had been proposed he quickly rose to the bait. 'Why not? Afraid you'll lose?'

'On the contrary,' said Holmes. 'But as a guest of the countess . . . '

'Don't let that stop you.'

'Very well,' Holmes said. He crossed to the wall, took down a matching sabre and slashed the air with it a few times. He then turned back to Howard, who was already removing his coat and shoulder holsters.

'I don't think this is a good idea,' Elaina said hastily.

'Neither do I,' said Watson. 'As much as anything else it's wildly irresponsible. No matter how careful you try to be, one or both of you is bound to sustain an injury.'

Holmes arched an eyebrow at Howard. 'What do you say? Shall we call it off?'

'Not a chance.' Howard cut the air with his sabre. 'I'm real curious to see how this pans out.'

'My sentiments exactly,' said Holmes. He quickly removed his jacket and passed it to Watson before bringing his blade up to salute his opponent.

'*En garde!*'

He and Howard circled each other, sabres extended, steel gleaming like liquid mercury in the gaslights. Watson wet his lips and felt his fingers digging anxiously into the material of Holmes's jacket.

Then Howard lunged forward, thinking to end the matter quickly and decisively. Holmes back-stepped, parried deftly and with a ring of steel Howard's blade slipped from his own. Howard himself stumbled forward, off balance, but caught himself quickly and leapt back to avoid a thrust from Holmes. He used his own blade to knock Holmes's aside, then moved in fast with a series of thrusts and swipes. But he lacked the finesse that Holmes displayed so ably, and as his temper warmed he lost even that small degree of ability and became instead a charging bull.

Holmes parried and countered, matching his opponent move for move, almost as if he knew in advance what Howard intended to do next.

They danced back and forth across the armoury, never losing eye contact. Then Howard lunged forward again and Holmes executed a deceptively simple twisting movement with his blade. It slid along the length of Howard's sabre and with another flick the American's sword flew from his grasp to land with a clatter on the flagstone floor.

Elaina gasped. 'There, it's done,' she said. 'And I declare Holmes the w — '

Neither man paid her any attention.

Holmes stood back and indicated that the Missourian should pick the blade up again. Howard did so, this time with murder in his eyes.

Again they faced each other. All of Holmes's needling had finally brought about the desired effect; Howard's temper, quick even at the best of times, had at last boiled over, while Holmes appeared to be as cool and collected as ever.

Howard leapt in. Steel clashed against steel. Howard lunged but Holmes sidestepped, eluding the other's sword. Again and again Howard hacked at Holmes, and in the end Holmes was forced to retreat under such a determined advance.

Elaina quickly stepped forward before Watson could restrain her and yelled: '*That's enough, do you hear me?*'

But her voice was drowned by the clashing ring of blade on blade. Holmes felt a wall at his back and knew he could retreat no further. Howard saw it as well, and heedless of the consequences brought his blade down in a sweeping overhead blow. Holmes dropped to a crouch before his opponent and the tip of Howard's blade ripped down the stone wall, splashing sparks from its tip.

Then, abruptly, Howard froze.

The tip of Holmes's sword was just

touching the soft flesh beneath his chin. One thrust and it would be all over for the man from Missouri.

'Do you concede?' asked Holmes.

'Never.'

'Then must we continue the match until one or the other of us is injured or worse?'

Elaina rushed in close, Watson following. 'My God, what're you two fools trying to prove?'

Without taking his eyes off Holmes; Howard said through gritted teeth: 'Respect has a price.'

'So does lying,' said Holmes.

Howard's anger flared and he backed away from Holmes's blade. 'Damn you, mister, you've gone too far now! No one calls me a liar!'

'Then what else does one call a man who was christened with one name and yet goes by another?'

'Holmes . . . ?' questioned Watson.

As he straightened up, Sherlock Holmes said: 'This man is not Thomas Howard. He goes by an altogether more celebrated name — that of the outlaw Jesse James!'

8

Grecian Fire

Tension continued to crackle between the two men. Then Howard — Jesse James, if Holmes was to be believed — reached a decision and tossed his sabre aside. 'Reckon there's no use in me denyin' it,' he said wearily.

'Not a bit,' Holmes replied.

Beside him, Elaina stared at Jesse in shock.

'When did you peg me?' Jesse asked Holmes. 'Where'd I slip up?'

'You didn't, Mr James.' Holmes set his own sabre aside. 'But the London *Times* carried your picture some six weeks ago. I recognized you as soon as I saw you.'

'How come you didn't call me on it?'

'I was curious to discover what had brought you to England. Your story of a missing younger brother was clearly a smokescreen. When I first questioned you on the matter, you were, to your credit, obviously reluctant to compound the initial lie with still more.'

'So why *am* I here?'

'I could make an educated guess, but I prefer not to indulge in speculation. I will leave it to you to explain.'

Before Jesse could reply, Elaina said in hushed disbelief: 'If you really are Jesse James, what *are* you doing here?'

'It's a long, grim story, ma'am. But maybe some of your fine British sippin' whisky'll make it easier to swallow.'

★ ★ ★

They left the armoury and returned to the library. After Fordham had served the drinks and left them alone, the man from Missouri began his tale.

'You know my name and you know my reputation. I ain't denyin' or makin' excuses for either. I've killed and robbed and though I ain't proud of it, I'll more'n likely do it all over again before I meet my Maker.'

He turned to Holmes. 'You were right when you said I had Welsh ancestry. My pa came from Wales. He was a Baptist minister . . . which I reckon makes what I've done all the worse. Still, we were raised decent, my brother Frank and me. It was the War taught us how to fight and kill and, after a fashion, how to live with the fightin' and the killin' afterward. We learned our lessons well. The

Unionists called us bushwhackers. We saw ourselves as guerrillas, fightin' stronger forces the only way we knew how, by hittin' them hard and then runnin' before they could mount a counter attack.

'Eventually we fell in with a feller named Bloody Bill Anderson, a cold-blooded killer who helped us hone our skills, if I can use such a word. After that, Frank joined up with an outfit known as Quantrill's Raiders, and later I joined him.'

'William Clarke Quantrill,' Holmes mused. 'I've read about him. He was responsible for a particularly blood-thirsty raid on Lawrence, Kansas, was he not?'

Jesse nodded. 'Yeah. But that was before I hooked up with him. You were right about somethin' else, too, Holmes. I *was* shot in the chest — on two occasions — and your miserable English weather *does* make those wounds act up . . . '

He paused, his mind drifting back to his early days. 'Anyways, after the war, times were hard in Missoura. Reconstruction robbed us of 'most all our rights. We couldn't carry guns, own slaves, work in government, not even preach . . . nor lawfully prevent Yankee carpetbaggers from commandeering our livestock or land. Only choice left us was to take what we needed by force.'

'Not everyone chose that road,' Elaina reminded him softly. Ever since she'd learned his real identity, she'd been studying him intently, sizing him up with fresh interest.

'True,' he admitted. 'And many folks would say me and Frank chose the wrong one. Maybe we did. Who's to know? All I can say is I sent letter after letter to the *Kansas City Times* — letters they published, too, to their credit — sayin' as how we were willin' to go straight, but still the law branded us outlaws.

''Course, I did a fair bit to deserve the name. I was always part of one gang or another, and we robbed banks and stagecoaches — even a fair, once — from Iowa to West Virginia and just about every place in between. A couple years ago we took to robbin' trains, as well.'

'And you gave some of the money to the poor, from what I've heard,' put in Elaina, 'which is why the newspapers began comparing you with Robin Hood.'

'It'd pleasure me to say that was true, Countess.'

'Ellie.'

'Ellie — but fact is, that whole 'Robin Hood' thing started 'cause one time there was some local families 'board a train we robbed and when Frank recognized them he gave 'em back their money. They spread the word and,

94

well, the press picked it up and made us sound like heroes. We all had a good laugh about it. Truth be known, there wasn't much profit in robbin' the poor. They got nothing worth stealin', anyway. So we concentrated on banks and the express safes, where the real money was.'

He chuckled, adding: 'Had a mighty good run of it, too. But finally the law got their fill of us, and one of the express companies hired the Pinks to run us to ground.'

'You're referring to the Pinkerton National Detective Agency, I take it?' said Holmes.

Jesse nodded. 'Their agents were everywhere. Got so bad, you couldn't cross the street in Kearney without bumpin' into a Pinkerton man.'

'Yet you were never caught,' Elaina said.

'No, ma'am. Kearney folk take care of their own, see. Wasn't no one ever gonna tell the Pinks where we was holed up. That was one of the things that got Cage Liggett so riled — he knew we were operatin' right under his nose but he couldn't get folks to turn us in.'

'Cage Liggett?' echoed Watson.

Jesse suddenly scowled, the mention of Liggett causing his temper to flare again. Gulping the remainder of his drink, he said: 'He was the man Allan Pinkerton chose to lead the hunt for me, the man I'm really here to find.' His eyes hooded dangerously. 'The man I'm here to *kill*,' he finished in a rasp.

Silence filled the room for long moments before Jesse found it within himself to continue. 'Cage Liggett's a hard, vain man, Mr Holmes, ambitious as hell an' cruel as winter. He promised Pinkerton that he'd have us in irons within two weeks of takin' the job, but Frank and me, we chose not to oblige him. 'Fact, we did all we could to lead him a merry chase and make him look the fool — and that was *our* mistake, I guess, for we should have stomped him the way you'd stomp any snake. But we didn't, and in the end he swore that if he couldn't catch us then he'd find some way to fetch us out into the open.

'Well, that Liggett eventually got so desperate, he started chasing rumours. And when one of his spies told him that me'n Frank planned on visitin' Ma and our stepdaddy, Dr Reuben Samuel, at the tail end of January just past, that was all Liggett needed to hear. He and a bunch of his men surrounded the house one night without being seen. They hid among the trees for a spell, tryin' to figure out what to do to flush me'n Frank out. Finally, accordin' to Liggett, he yelled for us to come out. Ma swears she never heard nothin' an' Ma's no liar. Anyway, when no one answered, Liggett threw a pot flare into the house . . . '

Holmes, seeing Elaina's puzzled frown, explained: 'Officially, it's known as Grecian fire. It resembles a lantern, except that it has a hemispherical cast-iron base and a brass top from which project two wicks. The idea is that the weight of the base makes sure the device always lands right side up, and its turpentine contents, which feed the wicks, act as a flare.'

'Well, that wasn't its purpose that night,' Jesse said grimly. 'Liggett used it as a bomb, hopin' to force us out into the open so him and his men could gun us down. 'Least, that's what his excuse was. Truth is, we heard that the Pinks got word at the last minute that Frank and me were fifty miles south, in Laurinsport.'

Watson swallowed hard. 'Are you saying this man Liggett *deliberately* firebombed your family home?'

'Damn right I am. I told you, he's a man of cruel temper, is Cage Liggett. We'd made him look the fool once too often, so he decided to pay us back by bombing Ma's house . . . '

He broke off, choked with emotion. Elaina wanted to go to him but wasn't sure how he would react.

Holmes said clinically: 'I wouldn't have thought

97

a pot flare would have caused that much damage.'

'Maybe not,' Jesse said, 'under normal circumstances. But the bomb rolled into the fire and exploded, blowin' off Ma's right arm from the elbow down and killin' my eight-year-old stepbrother, Archie.'

Again emotion choked off his words as he thought back to that night and imagined how it must have been in the long hours afterward; Ma sitting up all through the night, a cord tied clumsily around the stump of her arm to limit the bleeding; her weeping for her dying boy Archie; and two days — two whole days — before a doctor came and fixed her up as best he could.

First-hand memories came thick and fast, then, and what he visualized was so vivid and real he could feel the Missouri sun hot on his face; smell the ryegrass and hear the creaking of Ma's wagon as the mules pulled it up the slope from the foothills to the west.

'You were saying, Mr James?'

Holmes's voice brought him back to reality. Collecting himself, he explained that the day before he left Missouri, he and Frank had gotten word to their mother through a neighbour, telling her to meet them at the usual place around noon.

From the cover of some trees, they scanned Ma's back-trail with a pair of field glasses to see if she'd been followed. When they were sure she hadn't, they rode out of the wood and dismounted beside the wagon.

'Sorry we couldn't come to the house, Ma,' Frank said. He and Jesse shared a passing resemblance, but Frank's features were larger, his hair darker, his expression and demeanour more sober. 'But we heard the Pinks are still watchin' it day and night.'

'They are,' Zerelda Samuel confirmed. 'Fools don't think I see 'em, but they're easier to spot than a blind 'coon in the pantry. That's how come I know that cowardly pig-scum Liggett ain't with 'em.'

'He's gone, Ma,' said Jesse. 'Ol' Man Harris heard some Pinks talking in Blaine's feed store. Said when Liggett found out what happened to you and Archie, he took off.'

It was true. After word of the cowardly bombing had spread, Cage Liggett's name, along with that of Allan Pinkerton, the agency owner, became mud in most people's eyes. And as time passed, dark rumours started circulating that Liggett had better leave the country, and fast, because Jesse and Frank James were out to kill him.

'Reckon we'll never settle up with him now,' Zerelda said bitterly.

'Don't be so sure, Ma. Word is he's sailed for England.'

'England?'

Frank said: 'He's got a kid brother name of Jack who lives in a place called Liverpool. Gone to hole up with him.'

Zerelda frowned, her wrinkled, dried-up face bereft and toothless. 'Reckon we can forget about gettin' even, then.'

'England ain't as far as it sounds,' Jesse said. 'Not these days. An' it ain't *nowhere* near far enough to stop me from goin' after him.'

Zerelda's jaw firmed up. 'I still say you'll have more luck findin' sunshine in a blizzard.'

'It's already been decided, Ma. I got Liggett's picture, clipped it right out of the *Liberty Advance*. And I got plenty of money for passage and hotels. And when I get to this Liverpool place, I'll track him down. Count on it. And when I do . . . '

There was no need to finish the sentence.

Zerelda fixed him with eyes harder than granite. Then, with her remaining hand, she picked up the Bible from her lap and held it up to Jesse. 'Swear it to me, son,' she said. 'Swear, no matter what, you'll kill that gutless murderer.'

Without hesitation Jesse pressed his palm on the book. 'I swear.'

Satisfied, Zerelda returned the Bible to her lap, the movement making her wince.

'Arm still botherin' you, Ma?' asked Frank.

'Some,' she admitted, looking at the sleeve-covered stump. 'But I'm learnin' to do without it.' She reached down and gave each of them a fond, rough hug, then said: 'You're always in my prayers.' She then nodded to their black servant, Ishmael, and he clucked the horses back into motion.

Jesse and Frank watched the wagon as it descended the slope and disappeared into the trees. It was a sombre, silent moment. Then Frank took something from his saddlebag and handed it to Jesse. It was a pair of hand-tooled leather shoulder holsters.

'What're these for?' asked Jesse.

'Cole Younger reckons it's against the law for folks to go packin' iron in England, and I didn't want you goin' unarmed.'

Jesse grinned. 'Why, you miserable old sour-belly, damned if you ain't got feelin's after all.'

'If you're gonna get all mushy,' his brother growled, 'I'll take 'em back.'

But he was grinning as he said it, and Jesse was grinning too, and for a beat the brothers just stood there, neither wanting to say their goodbyes and go their separate ways. At last they hugged, briefly and self-consciously, and stepped back. Jesse hung the shoulder holsters over his saddle horn and mounted up. Frank grabbed the bridle and looked up at him.

'Jesse, promise me somethin'.'

'If you're worried about women . . . '

'Not women. Women I know you can handle. It's your temper, Jesse. Sometimes it's quicker'n a hair trigger. You get into trouble in England you won't have nobody to back your play.'

'Who says I'm gonna get *into* trouble?'

Frank's face was grim in the hard sunshine. 'You're lookin' to kill one, maybe two men, Jesse — I reckon that qualifies for starters.'

'Trust me, Frank. I can *do* this.'

'I know you can, little brother. But if you do get into a scrape — '

'Frank, quit your worryin'. I'll keep my temper and I'll stay away from the ladies. OK? As for England,' Jesse added, 'it won't throw a scare into me. It's got saloons and banks, and the folks there speak English just like us, don't they? How dangerous can it be?'

★   ★   ★

'How dangerous indeed?' echoed Holmes as Jesse finished his story. 'So you're here to find the man who maimed your mother and killed your stepbrother? A man you believed to have fled to Liverpool?'

'He *did* flee to Liverpool. I docked there myself not two weeks back and started showing Liggett's picture around, finally found a feller who claimed he talked to Cage an' Jack both in one of the saloons — pubs, I guess you call 'em — at the docks. They told him they were headed for London. So I went to the railroad depot where I 'persuaded' a ticket clerk to admit that he'd sold 'em tickets to a place hereabouts called Euston. I followed 'em there and after nosin' around I found out they spent a few nights at some kind of charity mission or hostel. Feller who runs the place said they were talkin' about goin' into business in what you folks call the East End. But that's where the trail went cold.'

'Curious,' noted Holmes. 'I should have thought that two Americans would have been easy enough to locate in that area.'

'They likely are,' Jesse agreed. 'But East Enders, they're like the folks back in Kearney — they clam up tight around outsiders like me. Could be you might have better luck.'

Watson looked scandalized. 'Surely you

don't expect Sherlock Holmes to help a known *outlaw?*'

'Why not?' asked Elaina. '*I* intend to help him.'

'Then do so by keeping him off the streets,' ordered Holmes. '*The Times* has a large circulation, and others will certainly have seen your picture. I also noticed a sketch artist here earlier from the *Illustrated London News*. Did he by any chance draw you, Mr James?'

'Yeah. But I took the drawin' away from him, plan to burn it later.'

'Well, that's good news.'

Jesse looked surprised. 'That mean you're throwin' in with us?'

'It means that I want you to stay undercover until I find this man Liggett and his brother. But I must also tell you this, Mr James. I am not entirely without compassion, and I will happily serve this man up to the authorities to pay for his crimes. But I will not serve him up to *you*.'

'But I promised Ma — '

'I do not care what you did or did not promise. I will not stand by and watch any man murdered in cold blood.'

Jesse glared at Holmes. 'Then let me tell *you* somethin': stay the hell out of my way, or you and me are gonna butt heads.'

'You're hardly in any position to make threats,' Watson reminded him.

'Then let's just say I'm givin' him fair warnin',' Jesse said. 'Same as I'd give anyone who tried to stop me from shootin' Liggett.'

'Well, I sincerely hope it does not come to that, Mr James,' said Holmes. 'For what it is worth, I do not believe all I read in the press. Now that I have met you and got your measure with my own eyes, I do not believe you are altogether the man you've been made out to be.'

'He means that as a compliment,' Elaina said as Jesse looked questioningly at Holmes. 'But he's quite right. You must stay here, out of sight, where I can hide you from all prying eyes.'

'Like you done this afternoon?' asked Jesse with a sour grin.

'This *afternoon*, cowboy, you were only suspected of rustling. How was I to know that in a matter of hours you'd graduate all the way up to being Jesse James?'

9

Mrs Violet Kidd

The offices of *The Era* were situated on the corner of Tavistock Street and Wellington Street. Holmes and Watson arrived shortly after opening time the following morning and were once again shown to the newspaper's archive, a dusty, almost forgotten room at the rear of the premises, which smelled faintly of mildew. Left alone, they each worked their way through one bound volume after another until, around noon, Watson said: 'Here — I think I've found it!'

Holmes was instantly beside him, peering over his shoulder at the small article headlined TRAGEDY STRIKES AERIAL-IST IN BRISTOL. Below the headline they read:

Mrs Violet Kidd, a member of the Tumbling Tornadoes aerialist act, presently in the employ of Castello's Circus, was injured in a fall during the evening performance at Castle Park, Bristol, on the 18th inst. The trapeze act went on about fifteen minutes after seven o'clock. The attendance at that time numbered around 500 persons, a large proportion of whom were women and children. A bungling with the ropes threw Mrs Kidd off balance at a crucial moment in her act and with great force she fell to the ground, breaking several bones. A scene of the wildest confusion followed. Ladies fainted, children cried and the crowd pressed forward towards the woman who lay senseless on the sawdust arena. But the active attendants of the show were too quick. Before the crowd could fairly realize what was done Mrs Kidd was transferred to the dressing-room and surgical aid sent for. In addition to some injuries of an internal nature, Mrs Kidd's left leg was fractured in several places.

'Well?' asked Watson. 'What do you think?'

'I think you have more than earned your keep today, old friend,' replied Holmes, noting the date of the story, which had happened some eight months earlier. 'At the very least we should discover what became of Mrs Violet Kidd.'

The bespectacled editor of The Era was more than willing to help. He confirmed that

Castello's Circus was still in business and after some searching through a box folder stuffed with various itineraries and schedules, announced that it was presently playing in Southsea, Portsmouth. Holmes thanked him and he and Watson headed for the nearest post office, where they sent a telegram to the owners, requesting the present whereabouts of Mrs Violet Kidd.

They returned to Baker Street and, while waiting for a reply, Holmes slipped into his long maroon dressing-gown and busied himself at his workbench.

He found relaxation in many varied hobbies, among them the study of Buddhism and the Cornish language and art, but perhaps his greatest passion was the study of honey-bees. It was no secret that Holmes was fascinated by the social order, behaviour and selfless work ethic of *Apis mellifera*. In fact, he often expressed his intention of one day retiring to the South Downs in order to keep them.

Now, as he studied the contents of one test tube or another and then scribbled notes, Watson asked him what he was doing.

'I am attempting to create a new allotropic form,' was Holmes's reply.

Watson pondered that momentarily, then said: 'Would you care to elucidate?'

'Certainly. As you know, every time a beehive is opened, cool sulphur smoke is used to cover the guards and induce a calming effect upon the workers, who are then encouraged by some arcane survival instinct to gorge upon honey. However, it has been my experience that the smoke can occasionally be noxious to the bees, and so I am trying to create a new, gentler allotropic form that is somewhat kinder to them.'

'I'm sure,' said Watson, returning to the newspaper, 'that all the little 'bumbles' will appreciate your efforts.'

Shortly after three o'clock the doorbell rang and soon thereafter they heard Mrs Hudson's tread upon the stairs. Holmes opened the door before she could knock and snatched the telegram from her outstretched hand. 'Thank you, Mrs Hudson,' he said, and promptly closed the door in her face. He tore open the envelope, unfolded the telegram inside and read it quickly.

'Excellent!' he said. 'According to the rather obliging Mr Andrew Castello, the last known address of Mrs Violet Kidd is here, in London — number Twenty-Seven Canal Road, Deptford. Watson, will you . . . ?'

'I know,' sighed Watson, rising from his fireside chair and limping towards the coatrack. 'Go downstairs and summon a hansom.'

★ ★ ★

The journey took just over half an hour. They crossed the Thames by way of Westminster Bridge and then the cab wound through the thin, mean streets of south London — Lambeth, the Elephant & Castle, Southwark and Bermondsey. The sun slowly began dipping westward, bathing the streets of tiny homes and dark, dusty shops in grey shadow. Eventually the cab slowed and the trapdoor in the roof behind them opened. The driver called down that they had arrived, adding: 'That'll be four an' a tanner, sir.'

Holmes gave him two half-crowns, then he and Watson climbed out to inspect their surroundings. In the fading light Canal Street looked derelict and isolated. The cobbled street was narrow, with a line of grimy terraced houses facing a peeling line of wooden palings and a murky canal beyond. Watson took one look at the houses, most of which appeared to have been boarded up, and said: 'I think we're too late. It looks as if the street has been condemned and everyone moved on.'

'Not quite everyone,' said Holmes, and

110

pointed toward the lamp-lit parlour window of a house right at the far end.

They walked toward it. Away to their right, scavenging rats squeaked and scurried between piles of refuse. Watson grimaced. He had been right about the other properties. They were all silent, and in darkness. Clearly Canal Street had been condemned, save for this one house — number twenty-seven.

Holmes rapped on the door, which badly needed repainting. After a few moments it opened and a small woman of about twenty-five peered warily around it. By the poor light they saw she had a pale face with tired blue eyes, a small, pointed nose and a thin, sad mouth. Her hair was a watery blond and pulled back in a bun, with an untidy spill of ringlets hanging as bangs. She wore a blouse buttoned to the throat and a full black skirt.

'Mrs Kidd?' asked Holmes.

She hesitated momentarily before saying: 'Y-Yes . . . Can I help you?'

'I believe you can, Mrs Kidd. I would like to question you about the events of two nights ago.'

She recoiled from him, her eyelids fluttered and she swayed dangerously. Watson recognized all the signs and pushed past Holmes so that he could catch her before she collapsed.

She slumped into his arms, and he was shocked by how thin and frail she was.

'Subtlety is not always your strong point, Holmes,' he grumbled.

At the sound of his voice the woman recovered enough to ask: 'Are you the police?'

'No,' said Holmes. 'And I should tell you at the outset that if you are honest with me, then the police will play no part in this.'

Mrs Kidd frowned at him. 'If blackmail's your game, you're wasting your time. We barely have enough for food and lodging.'

'We are not here to make your life any more difficult, madam. Quite the reverse — *if* you co-operate.'

She considered that for a moment, then nodded. 'I will,' she said. 'And if truth be told, it will be a relief to do so. Please, gentlemen, come in.'

As they stepped into a narrow passage, a weak, wheezy voice called out from the lamp-lit parlour. 'Vi? Is everything . . . ' The words were cut off by a prolonged fit of coughing. 'Is everything all right?'

She whispered: 'My husband, Emmanuel. He's ill, and sleeps downstairs in the parlour, where it is warmer.' Then, louder: 'Yes, Manny, it's all right.'

They followed her down the dark hallway, past a flight of stairs, until they reached a squalid little kitchen. She walked with a severe limp in her left leg, in just the manner Holmes had described in the grounds of Witton Abbey.

At last she gestured for them to sit at the wooden table. 'You're certain you're not from the police?' she said quietly.

'No,' Holmes said. Introducing himself and Watson, he added: 'We have been investigating a recent spate of jewel thefts, and I have come to the conclusion that you were responsible for their execution.'

She smiled bitterly. 'I can see it will do me no good to deny it.'

'No. But it may do you *considerable* good to tell me everything you know.'

'I will, sir. Honest. And as I just told you, I'll be happy to do it. I am not of larcenous character, gentlemen, and what I have done — what circumstances have forced me to do — has brought me great unhappiness.'

She fell silent for a while, as if bringing order to her thoughts. Then:

'You are right, Mr Holmes. I was born with a suppleness and balance that cannot be taught. My father spotted the ability in me when I was no more than five or six, and often took me into the city or to various racecourses, where I would walk a hastily erected tightrope or hang upside down from temporary railings for an audience who would, if the mood was upon them, give a penny or two in appreciation. I was a born performer, sir, it was all I ever wanted to do, so it was no hardship for me. But an unhappy home-life, caused mainly by my father's fondness for the bottle, eventually persuaded me that when I was old enough I would do as I had read in stories, and run away to the circus.

'This I did when I was fourteen. I found work with Castello's Circus, and began my real apprenticeship as part of an act called the Tumbling Tornadoes.

'Thereafter my life became one of constant travel. We played the provinces in all weathers, performing every day, all day. Throughout the racing season we could always be found at Epsom or Moulsey, Egham or Ascot. We even went abroad. And if we were lucky, we found work in pantomime at Christmas, which helped see us through the winter. It was a hard life, and one that put little money in one's pocket, but I loved it. I had wonderful friends, and more important, I had Manny.'

'Did he work for the circus?' Holmes asked.

Mrs Kidd nodded. 'He was as fine a juggler and plate-spinner as you have ever seen. He was also a dear, kind, gentle man. Despite the big difference in our ages, we were attracted to each other from the start. Manny was always considerate and loving, and when eventually he asked me to marry him I eagerly accepted. For two years we could not have been happier. Then he developed a bad, persistent cough and began to lose weight . . . '

Watson, who'd been listening intently, now murmured: 'Symptoms of consumption.'

'Aye,' Mrs Kidd said. 'Consumption it was. We had no money to treat him, but our employer was a good man. He paid for a doctor to examine Manny and gave us the use of a spare wagon. This meant Manny could still travel with us even though he could no longer perform, and I was able to nurse him when I wasn't on stage. But now that I was the sole breadwinner, I tried to make extra money by taking a more active part in the act. We incorporated a new element, a trick known as the 'Flying Leap for Life'. It involved jumping from one trapeze to another, performing one or more somersaults in mid-air and then being caught by a partner, who was hanging from the second trapeze. We rehearsed the trick a number of times without mishap, but for safety's sake, we retained a net to catch me in case I fell.

'The first time we performed the trick before an audience it went perfectly. But during a later performance that same day, disaster struck. As I leapt from my pedestal-board on to the trapeze, I felt the gearing shake and knew that for some reason the ropes to which it was fastened had come loose. I heard the crowd gasp with horror. Then one side of the trapeze dropped and I lost my grip. I landed on the edge of the safety net and was flung sideways, to the sawdust ring below. I broke my hip and ankle, and my career as an aerialist was over.'

Holmes arched a questioning eyebrow but didn't say anything.

'I was devastated,' Mrs Kidd continued. 'For now I had no means of earning the money that Manny and I needed to survive. And what else was I good for? The performer's life was the only one I had ever known. You can imagine my delight when, though the fall left me with a limp, I discovered that I still retained most of my abilities.

'Unfortunately, Mr Castello was of the opinion that audiences did not want to see a performer shuffling to and from the ring. It would remind them of the very real consequences when things go wrong, and the circus was there to provide an escape from such realities. I understood his reasoning perfectly, and could not argue against it.

'He gave me a small gift of money with which I managed to secure this property, and we have lived here, from hand to mouth, ever since. It has not been easy on me, Mr Holmes. But it has been far harder on poor Manny. He needs treatment, badly. But I could never afford to pay for it.'

'Until fate intervened,' said Holmes.

'Yes. I was returning from the grocer's one day when I sensed that I was being followed. Sure enough, I'd no sooner closed the front door when there was a knock. I answered it, and there stood a man I'd never seen before.'

'Did he introduce himself?' asked Holmes.

'He gave his name as Smith, but I fear it was an alias.'

'Was he a large man?'

'Yes, sir. Do you know him?'

'I know the prints he leaves beside riverbanks.'

'Well, he said that he'd heard how I once worked for the circus and was still quite a competent aerialist despite my injury. Hoping he might be from another circus, I said yes and invited him in. But he quickly dashed my hopes. He explained that he knew I was in financial difficulties, and might be able to help. But I had to be discreet, because his proposition was shady at best.

'I should have shown him the door at once, of course. I realize that now. But at the time, with Manny so sick and me at my wits end, I told myself that it would do no harm to at least hear his proposition.'

'Which was . . . ?'

'He said he was interested in a pair of earrings. He knew where they were kept but could not get to them, which is where I came in. He would take me to the property, I would gain access, steal the item and in return he would give me ten pounds.

'Well, it was a miraculous sum of money, and when I thought of all the good it could do my husband — I can make no excuses for what I did. I was simply desperate. So I embarked upon a series of robberies, the fourth and most recent of which was committed two nights ago.'

'This man Smith,' Holmes said, 'does he always take you to the scene of the robberies?'

'Yes, sir. He'd arrive unannounced with a sketch of the item he wanted me to steal and a five-pound note. I would receive the same amount again when I delivered the item to him.'

'And he never gave any indication as to the identity of his employer? Where he came from?'

'Never, sir. We rarely spoke of anything but the job at hand. He said it was better that way, for both our sakes.'

'Did he have a foreign accent?'

'No, sir. He was a Londoner through and through.' She dug out a soiled handkerchief and dabbed at her eyes. 'I have been a fool, sirs, and for that I will be eternally sorry. But the money has made Manny's suffering a little easier to bear, and though it may sound inappropriate, for that reason I don't regret my actions.'

Holmes frowned and pondered a moment. 'You have played a very dangerous game, Mrs Kidd,' he then said. 'Had you been caught, had you fallen and injured or killed yourself in the commission of the crimes, you would have left your husband in an even less enviable position than the one he already occupies. However, I understand why you embarked upon the course you did. But I suggest that you do not submit to this man Smith again, no matter how sorely you need the money.'

'He is an unpleasant man, Mr Holmes, and will not take kindly to a refusal.'

'Then tell him this, Mrs Kidd — that you received a visit from Sherlock Holmes, who warned you in no uncertain terms that the next time you committed a crime, he

119

would turn you over to the authorities. Tell him that I am on to him and if he has any sense he will keep a very low profile from now on.'

'I will do that, sir.'

Holmes rose. 'You have been a very foolish woman, Mrs Kidd, and I hope that from now on you will consider this a lesson learned.'

'I will, sir. And I thank you for understanding.'

'How is your husband at present, Mrs Kidd?' asked Watson, hearing another prolonged coughing fit.

'I fear he will not live to see out the summer,' she replied tearfully.

'Then clearly he needs more care than you can give him. It may be possible to remove him to an infirmary where — '

'Infirmaries cost money, Doctor.'

'Nevertheless, he needs rest, fresh air and nutrition if he is to stand any chance at all.' Watson hesitated before adding: 'It may be possible for me to arrange it, and in such a way that it will cost you little if anything.'

'Charity?' she asked disdainfully.

'Not charity, Mrs Kidd,' Holmes said. 'Let us call it payment for services rendered, for while your answers in themselves will not help me to solve the case, the fact that I have successfully deprived the real culprit of his most important tool — *you* — is worth far more than that.'

'You have done all that you can,' Watson said gently. 'But now your husband needs professional care. And I suggest you let me arrange it.'

'Very well, Doctor.'

'Excellent. I will have someone come for him tomorrow.'

Holmes picked up his hat. 'We must be going,' he said abruptly, uncomfortable as always in the presence of any show of emotion. 'Good night, Mrs Kidd.'

They left.

As they walked back through the darkness to their waiting cab, Holmes said: 'Tell me, Watson. Is it *really* possible for you to obtain free care for Emmanuel Kidd?'

'I doubt it. But I have some savings, and . . . '

Holmes smiled. 'You will carry the burden yourself, is that it?'

'Scoff if you like. But you were right. You told me not to judge the thief before I knew all the facts.'

'Then we shall share the cost of Mr Kidd's care between us, my friend. Your meagre pension of less than twelve shillings a day will only stretch so far, and while I may not be exactly wealthy, I am at least financially comfortable enough to go Dutch.'

Touched by his friend's generosity, Watson gave him a sidelong glance. 'You know, Holmes, there are times when you are as charitable as you are wise. But sometimes I question your wisdom. I mean, was it really wise to tell Mrs Kidd to tell this man Smith that you're on to him?'

'Quite,' said Holmes. 'I wanted to make sure the man left her alone. If he thinks that I may find him through her, he will give her a wide berth in future. If we are lucky, he will drop out of sight altogether.'

'But surely, he is the next link in the chain?'

'No. My feeling is that we are dealing with someone who leaves little to chance. Unless I am mistaken, this man Smith would have been hired through a whole series of other go-betweens. He will know very little in the grand scheme of things. But if word should get back to the *real* mastermind that I am on to them, we may yet smoke them out into the open.'

'Just like your bees, eh, Holmes?'

'Precisely.'

10

Obsession

Watson spent much of the following morning making preparations for Emmanuel Kidd to be removed to the St Marylebone Infirmary, where he knew some of the staff from his days as a student at the University of London. As he had predicted, a generous donation to the Nightingale Fund — the charitable organization which financed the infirmary — ensured that arrangements were completed swiftly.

He felt happy with himself as he limped back to Baker Street and collected the morning's mail from the hallway table. Consumption was not fatal in every case, and there was some evidence to suggest that a liberal diet of milk and cream, eggs, meat and vegetables — even raw eggs swallowed whole with a little sherry, pepper or salt on them — could boost the body's natural defences enough to fight it off. In the case of Emmanuel Kidd, however, Watson felt that it would be a long, arduous struggle. He could only hope that the man still possessed enough stamina to see it through.

There was no sign of Holmes when he let himself into their sitting room. He set his own post down on his chair and took the letters addressed to Holmes — and a rolled-up, dog-eared newspaper from America — across to his friend's bedroom door. Watson's room lay on the second floor. Holmes had his spartan sleeping quarters just off their sitting room, behind a door next to the fireplace.

'Holmes!' he called. 'The post has arrived!'

There was no response.

Frowning, Watson knocked on the door. 'Are you all right, old chap?'

Again, no answer.

He glanced around, looking for the note Holmes was sure to have left had he gone out. There wasn't one, and he felt a sudden stir of unease. Early on in their relationship Holmes had confessed to bouts of depression during which he would remain cloistered in silence for days on end. But those times normally were the result of inactivity, when he hadn't any interesting cases to occupy him. What if his friend were ill now?

'Holmes? Shall I bring your post to you?' he called through the door.

The silence was deafening. He turned away, trying to convince himself that his companion was merely sleeping late, as usual. But it was very close to lunchtime — late even by Holmes's bohemian standards.

He returned to the door, knocked and said: 'Holmes, are you all right? I'm coming in.'

He opened the door and poked his head inside.

Holmes's room was a study in basics. There was a single bed, a bedside table, a straight-backed chair, a tin dispatch box, and little else. Realizing that Holmes must have gone out, perhaps using his private exit set into the left-hand wall, Watson felt relieved. He turned to go, then froze.

'Good God . . . ' he murmured.

Holmes had covered one wall in photographs, newspaper and magazine clippings and what appeared to be whole reams of handwritten notes all pertaining to Elaina Montague. It was a virtual *shrine* to the woman.

Watson shook his head in amazement. It was in man's nature to seek a mate, of course, but in all the years he had known Holmes, he'd only ever shown true emotion for one woman, the American opera singer Irene Adler. To Holmes the female of the species was something to be tolerated, dealt with, observed, but never, ever loved. And yet here he had shown an interest in Elaina Montague that was more akin to obsession.

Not for the first time, Watson wondered just how well he really knew his companion. He knew very little of Holmes's personal life, just that he was descended from a family of country squires and had a brother named Mycroft, who was seven years his senior and was some kind of unspecified but clearly high-ranking civil servant.

From his own observations he had concluded that Holmes possessed all manner of eccentricities. Whilst scrupulously clean in himself, he thought nothing of keeping his pipe tobacco in the toe of an old Persian slipper and his cigars in the coal scuttle. What might appear as chaos to anyone else was Holmes's idea of order. And when presented with a new case he spared nothing, least of all himself, to solve it.

But between cases his spirits plunged and he grew lethargic and disheartened. At such times he sought comfort from cocaine which, he claimed, stimulated his mind. As far as Watson could see, however, it had entirely the opposite effect, and no matter how many times he saw it, the sight of the usually vital Holmes reduced in appearance to one of Homer's fabled lotus eaters, troubled him greatly.

'Have you quite finished gawping, Watson?'

Startled, Watson turned and saw Holmes

standing in the doorway behind him. He fumbled to find an answer. 'I'm sorry, Holmes. I didn't mean to . . . intrude. I came to deliver your post and when you didn't answer my knock I . . . ' Words failed him momentarily. 'I wasn't *spying* on you.'

Holmes tugged at the cuffs of his frock-coat. 'I never for one moment thought you were.'

'Good,' Watson said stiffly. 'Still, I have to say . . . all this gave me quite a shock.' He eyed Holmes questioningly. 'Old chap,' he said at last. 'Are you all right?'

'I have never felt better.'

'But . . . I mean, well, I knew you were interested in the countess, but *this* . . . ' he indicated the shrine of pictures and shook his head disapprovingly. 'It's not natural, Holmes.'

'On the contrary, Watson, under present circumstances it is *perfectly* natural.'

'Well, you know my opinion of that woman. I cannot possibly see the appeal.'

'Then let us leave it at that,' Holmes suggested. He extended his hand. 'My post, if you please.'

'What? Oh, yes. Here.' Watson turned and marched out, closing the door after him.

Holmes studied the envelopes, then tossed them aside and tore open the brown-paper sleeve around the newspaper. He sank on to his bed, unrolled the paper and quickly read the front page. Below the *Kansas City Star* banner, the headline read:

BRITISH NOBLEMAN MARRIES DANCEHALL QUEEN.

Below that there was a photograph of Elaina wearing a low-cut gown, and smiling as a much older man — Rupert, Earl Montague — presented her with a diamond necklace.

Holmes frowned. *Dancehall Queen?*

He read on:

According to the owner of the Empress Saloon, where Miss Corbin danced, the Count won her love with diamonds . . . .

'I'll just *wager* he did,' Holmes murmured.

He looked at the shrine, focusing on the newspaper clippings. Some were relatively new, others yellowed with age, but all showed pictures of Elaina and other women of her station — Lady Bingham, Baroness Alcott, the Duchess of Wakefield, Lady Darlington-White and others — taking tea at their homes and hers.

11

Entr'acte

The moment Elaina awakened the following morning she reached across the bed, expecting to find Jesse's naked, hard-muscled body stretched out beside her. When all she encountered was a cold sheet, she opened her eyes and saw that he was gone.

Disappointed, she sat up and looked around. It was still early, perhaps seven o'clock, but the sunshine was already making the lace curtains flare whitely and stretch shadows across the carpet.

'Jesse?' she called.

No answer.

'Jesse?'

Again no answer. At once she grew uneasy. He'd been in a grim mood after Holmes and Watson had left the previous evening, reluctant to entrust his search for the Liggett brothers to anyone but himself.

'Who's to say Holmes won't go straight to the police and tell them that Jesse James is in town, lookin' to kill two men?' he said, pacing angrily before the fireplace. 'You heard him. He ain't about to stand by and let me put a bullet in Liggett.'

Her face clouded. She'd known he wouldn't take kindly to captivity — even if it was for his own good and a very comfortable captivity at that. Neither did trust come easy to him. But if she didn't do something to calm him soon, she sensed that he might grab his belongings and walk out of her life, determined to kill the Liggetts and be done with it.

And that was the last thing she wanted to happen.

'You don't know Holmes or you wouldn't say that,' she chided. 'He's not perfect by a long way, but he is definitely honourable.'

'So you keep tellin' me,' Jesse snapped.

'Only because you won't listen to reason. Look,' she added gently, 'I know you're frustrated. And I don't blame you. I probably would be too. But the fact is Holmes apparently knew who you were from the start and yet he hasn't turned you over to police.'

'Yet,' Jesse muttered grimly.

Elaina sighed. 'All right,' she said wearily, 'for the moment, let's say you can't trust Holmes. At least trust me.'

'I do trust you,' he said. 'And don't think I ain't grateful for all your help, Ellie, but . . . '

Too frustrated to finish, he continued pacing.

She went to him, determined to continue the kiss they'd started earlier that day in the armoury. 'It's been a long day,' she soothed, 'and you're a fish out of water. You need an early night. It'll help you relax and sleep.'

Sensing her meaning, he took her in his arms and pulled her close. 'An 'early night' sounds like *just* what I need.'

Distracted as he was, he had been an ardent and attentive lover, and the sex had been pleasurable for both of them. But she knew that despite their lovemaking the restlessness in him had persisted; and now, this morning, he was missing and she was afraid that he might do something foolish.

Rising, she saw to her toilet and then dressed hurriedly in a white shirtwaist blouse, red twill skirt and high-top lace-up boots. Then she hurried through the house, asking the staff if they had seen Mr Howard. No one had, until she found Hallett, her groom, outside. He answered her question with a nod and pointed toward the stables, a row of box stalls beside the paddock. 'Last I saw him, m'lady, he was admirin' the horses.'

Elaina hurried to the stalls and stopped quickly when she spotted Jesse sitting in the first one, back to the wall, aimlessly toying with a bridle.

She sighed, relieved. About to warn him not to go off on his own again, she noticed the slump-shouldered, glum way he sat there and felt a sudden wave of compassion for him.

'Homesick?' she asked, kneeling beside him.

He grunted as if disgusted by his emotions. 'That obvious, huh?'

Her heart went out to him. Sitting beside him, she reached over and gently pulled him toward her, whispering: 'Nothing to be ashamed of. I get it all the time.'

'Sure you do. Who wouldn't want to swap all this for a few dried-up acres in Kansas?'

'Believe what you want, Jesse. But right now a little farm overlooking a cornfield sounds pretty good — so long as you're there with me.'

He set the bridle aside, turned to her and gently stroked her cheek. 'Shouldn't be talkin' that way.'

'Why not?'

''Cause there's no future hookin' up with a maverick like me. Hell, sometimes I think there's no future, *period*.'

'Nonsense! It's up to us to *make* a future. Together.'

'The Countess and the Train Robber, Jesse James. An interestin' pair *we'd* make. Hell, we'd be the talk of every town we lived in.'

'There are other things you could be besides a train robber.'

'Like farmer — sodbuster? No, thanks. Farming's what chased my daddy off to the California goldfields.'

'Your father was a prospector?'

'Farmer first, preacher second, prospector third.'

'That's an odd mix. Did he ever strike it rich?'

'No. Never even found enough dust to fill a single poke.'

'That's too bad. But he must have done well as a preacher. From what I've heard about the miners in the gold camps, they needed all the preaching they could get.'

'Maybe so. But they didn't get it from Pa. He only lasted a few months and then the fever took him.'

'I'm sorry.'

'Don't be. I was just a baby when he ran off, so his passin' didn't rip a hole in my heart. But it did learn me not to end up behind a plough.'

Elaina thought a moment, mulling over what Jesse had said. Then as if making a decision, she stood up and reached for his hand. 'Come on, *Mr Howard*. There's someone I want you to meet.'

'Not another Sherlock Holmes, I hope.'

'Far from it. You and Duke will get along just fine.'

She led him out into the early-morning sunshine. At the far end of the stables Hallett was mucking out another set of box stalls and replacing the bedding. She called to him and when he turned to her, she asked him to bring Duke out. 'I'd like him to meet Mr Howard.'

Hallett tipped his cap respectfully and entered the end stall. Moments later he led a pure white stallion out into the sunlight. Jesse whistled softly. By any stretch of the imagination the horse was magnificent. It stood seventeen hands at the shoulder and had a keen, knowing intelligence in its eyes.

The groom led the stallion up to Jesse, who eyed it admiringly.

'Now *this* is what I call a horse,' he said.

'Know a bit about horseflesh, do you, sir?' Hallett asked politely.

'I get by,' Jesse replied. He waved his hand before the horse's face, checking its vision, then examined its deep chest, withers, legs and hoofs.

'Come now, Mr Howard,' Elaina said mischievously, 'in your business, I would've thought that being able to choose a good horse was a matter of life or death.'

Jesse smiled, but said nothing. He focused his attention on the stallion, which now lowered its head and playfully prodded him in the chest.

Amused, Jesse fondled its velvety soft nose. 'Feelin'' pretty feisty this morning, are you? That's the trouble with stallions,' he said to Elaina. 'They look good, but they got a wild streak in 'em — unpredictable.'

'Like someone else I know,' she teased.

Jesse stood back, admiring the stallion's lines. 'OK,' he said at last. 'You got the looks. Let's see if you got any substance.' Taking the reins from Hallett, he grabbed the horse's long, flowing mane, swung up on to its bare back and kicked it into a gallop. The horse raced out of the courtyard, its drumming hoofs spraying gravel everywhere, and across the meadow beyond.

It was immediately clear that man and horse were in perfect harmony. Duke raced across the meadow with Jesse sitting straight-backed behind his big, pumping head. At the far end of the meadow he whirled the stallion around and brought him thundering back toward Elaina. At the last moment he swerved around her and continued on into a stand of ash trees. Seconds later he reappeared, the horse powering along under him, eyes wide, nostrils flared, mane flying. They raced back to the stables. Again gravel crunched underfoot as Jesse rode Duke back into the yard and performed a Pony Express dismount while the horse was still moving.

'I take it all back,' he said, handing the reins to Hallett. 'He's steady as a rock.'

Elaina looked at him through eyes that sparkled with hidden meaning. 'That's exactly what I wanted to hear,' she said.

12

Every Picture Tells a Story

Four nights later Charlie Poole, the fifty-year-old night-watchman at the three-storey Britannia Warehouse overlooking St Katherine's Dock, settled down for another quiet eight-hour shift.

He had no idea that it was to be his last.

Once Charlie had been a squat, brawny man with broad shoulders and knuckles as big and hard as chestnuts. He'd spent his early life fighting all-comers at the family boxing booth in Aberdare and in his time had fought hundreds of bouts, maybe more than a thousand.

Each and every one had taken its toll. His face was scarred, his nose flattened, his ears now great misshapen lumps of mangled cartilage clinging to each side of his head. All those punches had done something to his brain as well, slowing his thinking so that it became increasingly hard for him to grasp even simple things. Because of that his reactions had also slowed, and no one wanted to employ a boxer who couldn't hold his own against younger, fitter, hungrier club fighters, no matter how likeable he was.

So Charlie had been forced to move east and take this job at the warehouse. It was simple work. Most nights he settled comfortably beside the brazier in the far back of the ground floor and dozed the night away. Even the constant tattoo of rats scurrying from tea chest to tea chest had become like a lullaby to him.

Tonight he turned the bull's-eye lantern a little higher and unfolded the discarded copy of the *Illustrated London News* he'd retrieved on his way to work. He couldn't read very well but the *Illustrated London News* was just that — illustrated — and he enjoyed looking at all the pictures.

Nothing ever happened at the Britannia Warehouse, and he didn't expect that tonight would be any different. Settling the magazine on his lap, he took out an old knife and deftly peeled his nightly apple. This was another of his evening rituals — peeling the apple without stopping. At last the long spiral of mottled skin detached from the apple and he allowed himself a smile of satisfaction.

He was still good for something.

He heard another small, scuffling sound behind him. Bloody rats were more bold and restless than usual, he thought. He turned, intending to frighten them off . . . only to see that rats hadn't caused the noise.

He had a brief glimpse of a man in a black hood with a raised club in one hand and then . . .

The club smashed Charlie on the forehead and he spilled forward out of the chair, unconscious.

His attacker stood over him for a moment, admiring his handiwork, then took off his hood to reveal Jack Liggett. He whistled. Figures detached themselves from the shadows behind him — Alfie Adams, closely followed by Desmond O'Leary and Olwenyo Wadlock, pushing carts ahead of them.

'Start loadin' up,' Jack ordered. 'And don't miss nothin' or the Cage'll have your hides.'

As they set to work, Jack noticed the peeled apple. He picked it up and dusted it off, intending to take a bite, when something else caught his attention — the magazine the night-watchman had just been planning to read. He picked it up, angling it toward the lantern so that he could see the images reproduced there more clearly.

A moment later he swore softly. His brother needed to know about this — p.d.q.

★   ★   ★

139

Cage Liggett was stretched out on one of the two bunks that occupied the nine-foot-square living-quarters aboard the derelict barge they'd taken over shortly after reaching London. With its low ceiling and cramped combination of kitchen, day room and bedroom all rolled into one, it was a mean place that still stank of the coal and farm-produce it had once transported along Britain's canals. For many years it had more than earned its keep. Then, when it became cheaper to move goods by train, the scow had been abandoned and left to rot here along the eastern bank of the Thames, not far from the old fish market. At the time he and Jack had told themselves it was only temporary. But Liggett's dreams of getting rich quick had stalled and they were still stuck here.

As he often did, Liggett wondered if he'd been too eager to leave the States. If he'd stayed put and let Jesse James come to him the way the outlaw had threatened to, he might have been able to bushwhack him and reclaim some of his former reputation as a man to fear. As it was, he'd panicked, fleeing first to New York, and then, when rumours hinted that Jesse was closing in on him, to Britain. Anxious not to leave any kind of trail, he hadn't even told his brother he was coming. He'd merely

140

bought a passage under a false name and showed up in Liverpool. It had taken him several days to track down Jack, who had fled from New York where he was wanted for bank robbery, but once together again they had teamed up and started this life of petty crime.

But where had it got him, anyway? Much as he didn't want to believe it, it did seem as if Jesse James had followed them all the way here. The description Alfie and the others had given him was too close for comfort, but until he received confirmation, all he could do was lie low and fret.

He'd been fretting ever since the aftermath of the raid on the Samuel place. He had been so sure that it would force Jesse, with that hair-trigger temper of his, to throw his customary caution to the wind and come out of hiding. Then he'd show the sonofabitch!

But Jesse had decided to play a waiting game, and the waiting had sliced at Cage's nerves like a blunt knife.

He lost himself in memory then — and suddenly it was night in another country, and the tension within him was vying with an unholy sense of excitement and anticipation.

★   ★   ★

141

He'd given his men the order to dismount and then they'd crept forward, through the darkness, until the trees thinned and they were within sight of the Samuel place. It was a small one-storey wood-frame house with a front porch, flanked by a barn and a corral, built at the edge of the woods. Lights were on in the house and through the curtained windows he could see the silhouettes of people moving around in the parlour.

Liggett, by then aching for action, had taken out a cigar and lit it. Beside him, hunkered in the shadows thrown by the granary, one of his men had whispered: 'You sure you want to go through with this, Mr Liggett? I mean, what if Jesse and Frank really *are* in Laurinsport, like we been hearin'? Then all we're doin' is hurtin' his folks.'

'They're in there, all right,' Liggett had replied, though in truth he was now so keen to hurt the James boys any way he could that it didn't matter if they were in there or not. 'They always head back to their ma after a robbery, so they can brag about how smart they are.'

He'd edged forward to the corner of the granary and raised his voice. *'Jesse! Frank! We know you're in there, an' we got the place surrounded! Come out with your hands up an' no one gets hurt!*'

They waited, but there was no response, and a few moments later the windows went dark.

'They're gonna make a fight of it,' he whispered tautly. 'Well, that's just fine.'

Minutes passed. He and his men waited, watched, but nothing happened. After another five minutes he pulled the pot-flare from where he'd been cradling it beneath his jacket. It was wrapped in cloth and soaked in coal-oil. 'Pass the word,' he hissed. 'The minute Jesse and Frank come bustin' out, gun 'em down.'

'But that's *murder*, Mr Liggett!'

'No, Emmett, that's *justice*. The James boys've made a fool of me once too often, an' I don't intend for 'em to do it again tonight. Now, pass the word, goddammit!'

He touched the glowing tip of his cigar to the end of the bomb's two fuses, waited for them to burn a little, then crept in closer until he was near enough to hear the muted conversation coming from within the sitting room.

The last thing he heard before he hurled the bomb through the kitchen window was the sound of a young boy, giggling.

The sound of shattering glass sounded much louder than it should have. Immediately there was a commotion from inside, the sound of running feet. A moment later there came the dull thump of an explosion that shook the ground and shattered the rest of the windows.

The pot-flare had exploded and though he didn't know it at the time, a shard of it slammed right through young Archie Samuel's chest. Jesse's ma, Zerelda, screamed as her right arm was torn off.

Realizing then that this probably *had* been a step too far, Liggett had scurried back to the trees, where he watched the woman, clutching the remnants of her arm, her husband Reuben, and their Negro servant come outside.

There was no sign of Jesse, no sign of Frank.

There was, however, more screaming and shouting when they discovered that the back of the house was alight and the flames were spreading fast. He learned later that the pot-flare had also ignited the supply of kerosene in the Samuel pantry.

He and the others had watched them struggle to put the fire out. No one said a word, or moved to help. It was done, and there was no undoing it. The best he could hope for now was that the public was so sick of Jesse's shenanigans that they would see this attack on his family as a good thing.

They didn't.

In the weeks that followed, Zerelda Samuel told anyone who'd listen that the plan had been to kill everyone in the house and let it burn to the ground, destroying such evidence as there was; the public, the same gullible public who'd been on the receiving end of Jesse's depredations all this time, believed her.

As a wave of sympathy for Jesse and Frank had swept the state, Cage Liggett's name became mud. He'd thought Allan Pinkerton and the public at large would applaud him for taking the fight to Jesse. Instead the opposite had applied. Worse, Jesse had let it be known that Cage was going to have to answer to him for what had happened, and soon.

★   ★   ★

The sound of footsteps hurrying down the ramshackle wharf interrupted his thoughts. He grabbed the horn-handled knife that had once belonged to Blackrat Lynch, hid behind the door and prepared to strike.

But it was only his brother, who jumped back as Cage lunged at him.

'Whoa, hold it!' Jack exclaimed. 'It's just me. But you might like to keep that blade handy,' he added, ''cause you're gonna need it.'

'What does that mean?'

Jack threw the *Illustrated London News* on to the table.

Liggett picked it up and looked at the page it was folded to. It was the society page, a report of a social gathering headlined AMERICAN VISITOR THRILLS GUESTS AT MONTAGUE MANSE. Several engravings accompanied the article, each depicting one important guest or another. But it was to the illustration of a man spinning a lasso over his head that Jack pointed.

Cage looked a little closer, then closer still. A cold knot of dread suddenly tightened in his belly.

It was unmistakably Jesse James, named in the caption below as 'Mr Thomas Howard from Missouri.'

Liggett angrily stabbed the knife into the table top. 'It's true, then! Some sonofabitch Pinkerton must've ratted me out!'

'Sure looks that way,' Jack agreed grimly. 'But it don't make sense. If Jesse's come all this way to kill you, why the hell's he performin' rope tricks and havin' his picture drawn?'

'I dunno,' Liggett growled. 'And I don't care. Only thing that matters now is that we get *him* 'fore he gets *us*.'

'Us?' countered Jack. 'What's he want to kill me for? I ain't even met him.'

''Cause you're my goddamn brother! That's more'n enough reason for Jesse. Hell, Frank had to stop him from shootin' one of the Daltons for laughin' when Jesse's horse threw him.'

Jack paled and said: 'Then we better find a way to ambush the bastard, quick.'

Liggett shook his head. 'No. Where Jesse's concerned, even an ambush is too risky. If somethin' went wrong an' he got a chance to draw his guns . . . ' Leaving the rest unsaid, he lay back on his bunk and tried to think.

Outside, the river current gently swelled. The old barge creaked and groaned as rippling water slapped against its sides.

'Maybe we should make a run for it,' Jack said. 'Europe's an easy place to get lost in.'

'So's the North Pole, but I ain't goin' there!'

'All right then, what about Australia? I've heard it's got lots of open spaces. And cattle and sheep ranches run by wranglers and cowboys.'

'Yeah, an' they're all escaped limey convicts,' Liggett said. Then an idea hit him and he sat up, saying: 'I got it!'

'Got what?' Jack said, eagerly leaning forward.

'How we'll fix Jesse.'

'I'm listenin'.'

'We'll frame the no-good bastard.'

'How?'

Liggett said only: 'Trust me, little brother. We're gonna turn us a handsome profit and let Scotland Yard take care of Mr Thomas Howard in the process.'

13

Stick-Up!

The new day's business was already under way, and the Square Mile — that district at the very heart of London dominated by the city's financial institutions — was bustling. Office workers hurried to and fro, dodging omnibus, growler and hansom cab alike in order to cross from one side of the narrow cobbled streets to the other, and sweepers were already out in force, fighting their never-ending battle to keep the streets clean of manure.

The pace of life was frantic and noisy, as befitted the capital of the world's trade and commerce. Consequently, few people paid much attention to the five riders dressed in buttoned-up cotton dusters and dark, wide-brimmed Stetsons riding their horses casually along Jewry Street. They eventually dismounted — two more expertly than the rest — outside the city branch of the Crosbie & Shears bank.

As four of these men passed their reins to

the fifth, a little man who kept sniffing and wiping his runny nose, their eyes seemed to be everywhere at once. Although the morning was bright and dry, the street was bathed in shadows, for the sun rarely found its way down between the tall, red-brick buildings to ground level. After some moments the leader gave an authoritative nod. As one, all but the designated horse-handler covered their faces with neckerchiefs and entered the bank.

As they burst through the doors into the large, ornate main room, dusters flapping around their calves, boots clattering over the tiled floor, clerks and customers whirled around in surprise.

Drawing revolvers, the robbers covered everyone.

'You,' the leader snarled at the customers, 'get down on your faces!'

Panicked, they obeyed, the women among them screaming. One, an elderly matron, paled and stood there a moment, close to fainting. The men stiffened. One of them took a defiant step toward the robbers. The leader pistol-whipped him, sending him sprawling.

'Next one of you don't do like I say gets a bullet!' the leader growled. 'Now, all of you — on the floor, goddammit!'

As the customers obeyed, the leader turned to the startled cashiers standing behind the counter with their hands up. 'You fellers hand over all your paper money and nobody gets hurt, understand?'

Some of the cashiers nervously nodded, others stared wide-eyed at the robbers. For another long moment no one moved. The leader raised his weapon and aimed it at the nearest clerk, a thin-faced young man with oiled black hair and dark eyes. 'You *hear* me, jerk-head?'

The clerk stared back at him, suddenly showing more anger than fear. He started to protest, but before he could say anything the manager appeared from a doorway behind him. 'Do as he says, Martin!' he ordered. 'You other fellows as well!'

Immediately the cashiers emptied out their cash drawers. The other gang members stepped over the prostrate customers and produced gunnysacks into which the money was dropped.

The leader looked toward the doorway. Outside, the horse-handler was still checking the street in both directions and occasionally wiping his nose.

So far their luck was holding.

'Hurry it up, you morons!'

The robbers grabbed the now-filled gunnysacks and hurried to the front door. The leader, guns still covering the customers and bank staff, slowly backed up after them.

'We're goin' now, folks. Anybody tries to follow us gets a ticket to hell.'

As he turned to leave, one of his men whispered loudly: 'Wait! What about the safe, Jesse?'

'Shut up, you fool!' the leader hissed. 'Now they all know who I am!'

The man cringed, as if fearing a bullet, and ducked out through the doors. The other men quickly followed.

Alone, the leader gave a mocking salute to the customers and bank staff. 'The James boys thank you, ladies an' gents!'

Taking aim at the big crystal chandelier hanging from the centre of the domed ceiling, he fired twice. The chandelier shuddered as the bullets broke the chains and then dropped to the tiled floor, shattering on impact. Crystal shards flew in every direction, bringing more screams from the women.

A moment later the leader was gone, vaulting in to his saddle and riding off with his men.

★　★　★

It was lunchtime when Watson bustled into their Baker Street lodgings. 'Holmes,' he exclaimed, joining his friend at the window.

152

'Holmes, you'll never believe what's happened!'

'The bank robbery, you mean?'

Deflated, Watson threw his copies of *The Times* and the *Graphic* on to a chair. 'You've already seen the papers, I take it?'

'No. But as you will observe, the window is open and I have heard the cries of the paperboys selling their wares. I have only been awaiting your return so that we might deal with the matter together.'

'Well, you don't seem at all surprised.'

'I'm not. I have been expecting such a turn.'

Watson shook his head disparagingly. 'I *knew* we couldn't trust that fellow.'

'Once a thief, always a thief, eh?'

Watson scowled at the implied criticism. 'I am willing to concede that in the case of Mrs Kidd I was mistaken. But Jesse James has been an outlaw for years. His is clearly a recidivist nature. Besides, you cannot argue with the facts.' He gestured to the discarded newspapers. One headline read JAMES GANG ROBS LONDON BANK, the other JESSE JAMES TERRORIZES LONDON. Below each headline was a picture of Jesse.

'And these are 'facts'?' asked Holmes.

'As presented by the people who were there, yes.'

'Then may I suggest that all is not necessarily as it may appear? Aside from anything else, Jesse James is here to settle a very personal matter with the Liggetts. I do not think he would endanger that mission upon such a whim, no matter how recidivist his nature. For another matter, there were five robbers in total. Where did he recruit his four companions, especially at such short notice? No, Watson — Jesse James definitely did *not* commit this crime.'

'Then who did?'

Before Holmes could reply there was a knock at the door. 'Come.'

Mrs Hudson appeared. 'I'm sorry to disturb you, Mr Holmes, but that dreadful boy Wiggins has just left you a message.'

Holmes was immediately attentive. 'Which is . . . ?'

' "No joy",' she replied.

Holmes nodded, clearly disappointed. 'Thank you, Mrs Hudson.'

Watson, who'd had time to answer his own question, waited for the landlady to leave, then said: 'Holmes, are you saying that this robbery was the work of the Liggetts?'

'I am saying that that is certainly more plausible than the alternative,' Holmes replied. 'But what say we ascertain the truth of the matter for ourselves? Let us see. The robbery was committed in Jewry Street, which puts it squarely in the jurisdiction of the Seething Lane division of the City of London Police. That makes it the responsibility of Inspector Varney — a competent if occasionally short-sighted investigator.'

'By all means,' Watson said. 'Lead on.'

★ ★ ★

They arrived at Seething Lane police station just as Inspector Jacob Varney was donning his overcoat and preparing to leave. The big, bearded policeman looked up when they were shown in and, though in a hurry, took a moment to shake their hands warmly.

'This is an unexpected surprise, and no mistake,' he said. A man of average height and considerably overweight, he was about forty and seemingly incapable of looking anything other than dishevelled. 'What brings you here, Mr Holmes? And you'd better be quick. I'm off to catch a criminal.'

'Has there been a breakthrough in this morning's robbery?'

'Let's just say that I'm confident of an arrest,' said Varney. He shook his head in wonder. 'You know, I didn't even suspect that James fellow was in the country! But it will do me no harm to be known as the man who brought him to heel.'

Holmes smiled sardonically. 'With the help of an anonymous tip-off, no doubt?'

'What do you know about that?' Varney asked suspiciously.

'May I see the message?'

Varney hesitated, then grudgingly picked up a manila folder from his cluttered desk and handed it over. Holmes opened the folder to reveal a single sheet of thick, cream-coloured notepaper. The white envelope in which it had arrived was affixed to the letter by a pin. It had not been sealed with wax; the flap had merely been tucked into the body of the envelope. The message was written in neat, careful capitals:

THE OUTLAW JESSE JAMES IS HIDING OUT AT COUNTESS ELAINA MON-TAGUE'S RESIDENCE IN RICHMOND.

It was signed, *A CONCERNED CITIZEN*

'Thank goodness for the great British public, eh?' said Varney. 'They'll never let you down.'

'This is the work of an American,' said Holmes.

'Eh? How the dickens can you tell that?'

'The turn of phrase,' said Holmes. ''Hiding out' is an American term. We would simply use the phrase 'in hiding'. By the way,' he added, 'when was this delivered?'

'Not twenty minutes since. And before you ask, sir, no; the desk sergeant *didn't* see who delivered it.'

'And yet you still insist on acting upon it?'

'I can't afford not to, sir.'

'True. But you *do* know it is just a ruse — a red herring to throw you off the scent of the real perpetrators?'

'I know no such thing, sir.'

'Tell me what you know about the robbery, Inspector.'

Varney was about to remind them that he was on his way out, then thought better of it. After all, this was Sherlock Holmes, a man for whom he had the greatest respect. Besides, he had an uneasy feeling that he might need Holmes before this case was closed. Briefly he reported the facts as they had been given to him by the witnesses.

'So, just to clarify the matter,' said Holmes, 'at least two of the robbers spoke with an American accent, and the manager and staff were able to deduce their identity first by one of them letting slip the name 'Jesse' and then by the man, Jesse, referring to himself and his men as 'the James boys'?'

'Correct,' said Varney.

'Doesn't that strike you as being somewhat

. . . clumsy? Even obvious?'

'Not necessarily, sir. We all let things slip in the heat of the moment.'

'Then why did they go to the trouble of wearing masks?'

'Old habits?'

Holmes's thin mouth narrowed still further. 'How much was stolen from the bank?'

'Close on a thousand pounds, sir.'

'Then the reward for information leading to the arrest of the culprits and the return of the money would generate a reward of not less than one hundred pounds.'

'That's quite correct,' the inspector confirmed.

'And yet your informant prefers to remain anonymous, and forgo what is a considerable amount?'

'Perhaps he has a social conscience, sir. Perhaps bringing this criminal to heel is reward enough.'

'Or perhaps he is just out to make mischief, and cause the countess no small embarrassment.'

'The countess,' Varney said distastefully. 'We all know about *her*.'

'We have all heard the *rumours*,' corrected Holmes.

'Yes, rumours. But it's my experience that where there's smoke there's fire, Mr Holmes.

Could a woman of that type knowingly harbour a criminal? I do not think it beyond the realms of possibility. So I have to check it out.'

'Naturally. All I ask is that you use discretion, Inspector. The countess is a friend of mine and I should not like to see her distressed by this slur.'

'I will be the very epitome of discretion,' Varney promised, pronouncing the word as *eppy-tomey*.

'I would ask one other favour,' Holmes said. 'That we accompany you.' When Varney hesitated, he added: 'A friendly face may encourage the countess to co-operate more fully.'

Varney, realizing the sense in that, said: 'Quite what I was thinking. Certainly you may accompany me, Mr Holmes. I should be glad of your assistance. Now, if you'll give me a moment to arrange some transport . . . '

He hurried from his office and started bellowing orders.

Watson said quietly: 'Do you think it was wise to offer to accompany him? I mean if James really is innocent, as I am now willing to concede, then we have to forewarn him. We could have slipped away and sent a telegram, perhaps, or — '

'No, Watson. If the telegram were to come

159

to light at some later stage it would implicate us in perverting the course of justice. And though I have been known to follow my own counsel in times past, neither of us would choose to do that willingly. We must hope that the countess and Jesse James both are as sharp-witted and resourceful as we believe them to be.'

Varney lumbered back into the room. 'Are you ready, gentlemen? There'll be a growler and a black Maria wagon around the front in ten minutes.'

14

The Search

For the next hour or so the three of them were cooped up together inside a four-wheeled carriage. Behind, two sturdy draught horses pulled a black Maria wagon crowded with uniformed constables.

It was mid-afternoon when they wheeled up before Montague Hall. The butler showed Varney, Holmes and Watson into the library, where Elaina waited for them beside the fireplace. She looked elegantly stunning and, at first, delighted to see them. Then as she heard the inspector's request to search her premises, she became shocked.

'Surely, Inspector, you must realize that the very *notion* that I would entertain a known criminal here, much less hide him from the authorities, is ludicrous.'

'Of course, m'lady,' Varney said deferentially. 'And naturally I apologize for the inconvenience. But I have to act upon all information received. And that is why I must ask your permission to search the house and outbuildings.'

Elaina looked at Holmes. 'Is this *your* doing, Mr Holmes?' she asked angrily.

'No, Countess. In the first place, there is nothing to suggest that Mr James is even in the country, much less that he has committed any crime. I am of the opinion that someone is attempting to lead the police investigation astray, playing a rather *im*practical joke, or simply hoping to embarrass you.'

She smiled at him, and he and Watson both saw the relief in her eyes. Holmes hadn't betrayed Jesse, then — not that she had believed he would. But Jesse himself had been so convinced. Then again, trust must come hard to a man who had lived the life he had. She couldn't blame him for his misgivings.

Still, it had been a close-run thing. It was Jesse, on edge ever since they had heard news of 'the James boys' robbery, who had first sprung from his chair as if poked with a stick, Jesse who had been alerted by the faintest tinkle of harness even as the two police coaches appeared around the line of trees, heading along the drive at a determined trot.

'You expectin' someone?' he'd asked her.

'No.'

'They're policemen, ain't they?'

'Yes.'

'Damn that Holmes! He's sold me out!'

'No, Jesse, you don't know th — '

'Well, I ain't surrenderin' without a fight!'

'No, no. Please. No gunplay!'

'I got no choice,' he said. Angrily, he indicated the afternoon edition of the newspaper lying on the table. 'I ain't confessin' to a crime I didn't commit.'

An idea hit her. 'Maybe you do have a choice . . . ' She tugged on the nearby bell-pull and within moments Fordham knocked and entered. 'Yes, my lady?'

'I want you to take everything from Mr Howard's room and hide it.'

The butler's only response was an infinitesimal lift of the eyebrows.

'The police are about to arrive, and I suspect they believe that Mr Howard was somehow involved in this morning's robbery of Crosbie and Shears.'

'But Mr Howard has been here all day, my lady. I would be more than willing to testify to that.'

'Thank you, Fordham, but for reasons I can't explain that won't be enough. Now, please do as I ask. Oh, and instruct the staff not to mention that Mr Howard was ever here.'

'Very good, my lady,' Fordham said without hesitation. Then as they heard the coaches pulling up outside, he added: 'I will answer the door, my lady, and then attend to it.'

'Thank you. But hurry. I'll only be able to stall them for so long.'

As Fordham hurried out, Jesse said: 'What about me? I ain't as easy to hide as a suitcase.'

'This is a large estate. Go find someplace on the grounds to lie low and don't show yourself again until the police are gone.'

'I can't do that,' Jesse said. 'If they find me, it'll implicate you. And believe me, you wouldn't like being on the wrong side of the bars.'

'Then make sure they *don't* find you,' Elaina said. She pulled him close, kissed him passionately and then pushed him towards the French windows. 'Go on, darling. Do as I say. *Now!*'

Jesse left.

Now, in answer to Varney's request to search the premises, she said: 'I gather you have a search warrant, Inspector?'

'No, m'lady,' he replied. 'But I can get one, if needs be. I was rather hoping it wouldn't come to that.'

'It doesn't have to,' Elaina said. 'I give you my personal assurance, Inspector, that you will not find the man you seek — always assuming he actually *exists*, that is — here.'

164

'I appreciate that, m'lady. But I still have to check.'

'Then my word isn't good enough?'

'I never said that, m'lady. And I'd be obliged if you didn't go putting words in my mouth. Now, do we have your permission or not?'

Elaina hesitated, still stalling for time. No one would blame her for insisting upon a warrant. But then there came a knock at the door and she said: 'Enter.'

Fordham came in. 'Will the gentlemen be staying for tea, my lady?' he enquired. His bland expression gave nothing away, but as soon as the opportunity presented itself, he gave a brief but unmistakable wink that only she caught.

Hiding her relief she said: 'Will you, Inspector?'

'Thank you, m'lady, no.'

'Dr Watson and I would enjoy a cup,' Holmes said to Elaina. Then to Varney: 'I'm sure you and your men are quite capable of making a thorough search without our help.'

'Quite,' said the Inspector.

'Fordham,' said Elaina, 'Inspector Varney and his men will be conducting a search of the house. Please give them every assistance.'

'Yes, my lady,' Fordham replied, and left.

Thanking her, Inspector Varney promised

to be as quick as possible, and be the very epitome of discretion. Once again he made the word sound like *eppy-tomey*.

As the inspector left to organize the search, Holmes said quietly: 'Have no fear. I doubt the police will find him unless he is exceptionally clumsy.'

She frowned. 'What makes you say that?'

Ignoring the question, he went on: 'You know, of course, that the Pinkerton agent, Cage Liggett, was behind the robbery at the bank, his plan being to incriminate James so that the police would deal with him?'

'Of course.'

'If your staff are questioned, can they be trusted not to talk?'

'They will say nothing,' she assured him. 'I may be many things, Holmes, but never a bully. I've always treated the servants well, and they in turn have given me their complete loyalty.'

'Let us hope you are right, Countess. If Varney finds James, or if your staff let something slip, you will be ruined. Harbouring a known criminal, especially one of James's calibre ... the courts will not be inclined to leniency, I fear.'

Varney waited in the hallway while his constables went through the house from top to bottom. The attic was opened and

166

inspected. Every room was unlocked, underneath every bed was checked, every cupboard and wardrobe opened and scrutinized. The cellar was examined, and then the stables, the outbuildings, even the little crooked row of staff cottages.

Last of all the grounds themselves were searched. Elaina waited tensely beside Holmes and Watson, expecting at any moment Varney to enter the room and grimly tell her that James had been found and apprehended, and it was time for her to admit that she'd been harbouring a criminal all along.

But the long, tense minutes continued to be marked by the metronomic ticking of the spelter clock, and nothing happened except more waiting.

The search took over an hour. But at last Inspector Varney entered the library, his expression sheepish. 'Thank you, m'lady. I'm sorry to have troubled you.'

With effort, Elaina hid her relief and, with a glassy smile replied: 'That's quite all right, Inspector. You were only doing your duty.'

'Very decent of you to see it that way, m'lady.'

'However,' she added, 'my lawyer, Sir Ashley Danvers-Cole, will hear about this when I next see him.'

Varney, familiar with the lawyer's fearsome

reputation, looked crestfallen. 'Yes, m'lady,' he said meekly. And then, to Holmes and Watson: 'Are you coming along?'

'No,' Holmes said. 'The countess has kindly invited us to dine with her.'

With a nod, Varney made one final apology and then left, thoroughly shamefaced. From the library window they watched as his men climbed into the back of the black Maria wagon while Varney himself squeezed into the growler. A moment later they were heading back down the drive.

'Heaven knows where Jesse went,' said Elaina, turning to Holmes. 'He could be miles away by now.'

'I think not,' Holmes replied. He stepped to the French windows, let himself out on to the terrace, and descended the stone steps into the gardens themselves.

Elaina raised her eyebrows at Watson. 'Now where's he off to?'

Watson shrugged. 'May I suggest we follow him and find out, my lady?'

With purposeful, long-legged strides Holmes headed for the giant oak which stood in the centre of the wide, spacious lawn. Upon reaching it, he stopped and called: 'You can come down now, Mr James.'

Nothing happened.

'I assure you that Inspector Varney and his

men have left. You have nothing to fear.'

The branches shivered, and as Elaina and Watson approached they saw Jesse climbing down through the tangled foliage. Dropping lithely to the ground, he stretched to ease the kinks from his spine, then confronted Holmes.

'All right,' he said grudgingly. 'How'd you figure out I was up there?'

'Elementary,' Holmes replied as the others joined them. 'When one is searching, one will look from left to right and round about, but rarely will one ever look *up*. And though you are clearly an excellent climber, sir, you are also of sturdy build. As you climbed, you dislodged a number of leaves. Since it is hardly likely that an oak, which is in full bloom by this time of year, would shed its leaves at any time before October, it was therefore logical to assume that something or someone of substance was in the tree.'

'Hell's fire,' Jesse grumbled. 'Don't you ever get tired of beating your own drum?'

'You asked the question, Mr James. I merely provided the answer. But now I suggest we go indoors. Should the inspector happen to return for any reason, it would not bode well for the countess if he were to find you here. Besides, we have much to do if we are to clear your name and bring the real culprits to book.'

Jesse frowned, surprised. 'Then you don't figure I was part of that hold-up?'

'Of course not. Unless we are both very much mistaken, it was Cage Liggett.'

'The man you said you could find,' Jesse reminded him sourly.

As they all walked back to the house Holmes said: 'For the past four days I have had my agents, whom Watson refers to as my Baker Street Irregulars, scouring the East End in search of the Liggett brothers.'

'The Baker Str — what the hell are they?'

'A band of street arabs,' said Watson. 'Urchins led by a lad named Wiggins who . . . ' He broke off suddenly as he remembered the message Mrs Hudson had given Holmes shortly before they'd left for Seething Lane. 'So *that*'s what Wiggins's message meant!' he exclaimed. 'He's had 'no joy' in finding the Liggetts!'

'Precisely,' said Holmes. 'And so it falls to me to make enquiries in person.'

'Don't worry,' Elaina said as she saw Jesse looked doubtful. 'Holmes *will* locate them. I'd bet my life on it.'

'Sure hope you're right,' Jesse said. 'I don't mean to sound ungrateful, Ellie. You and your servants have done right by me and I truly

170

appreciate it. But I reckon I've kicked my heels 'round here long enough. If you don't turn the Liggetts up soon,' he added to Holmes, 'I'll have to do the job myself.'

'That would be a grave mistake,' Holmes said. 'You'll go blundering into the East End and more than likely get yourself killed or arrested. Don't forget, the Liggetts know you're here now, Mr James. I don't know how — perhaps that sketch artist from the *Illustrated London News* made another drawing of you when you weren't looking. But this much is certain — you have lost the element of surprise and they are out to get you before you can get them.'

'Let 'em try,' Jesse said. 'They'll learn to regret it. I've made a promise and I aim to keep it. I'm gonna kill those sorry bastards, Holmes — an' *anyone else* who tries to stop me.'

'Jesse, please,' Elaina began.

He cut her off, temper flaring. 'You're wastin' your breath, Ellie. I'm at the end of my rope. If Holmes don't find Liggett by tomorrow, I'll track him down myself.'

15

A Tempting Offer

Despite telling Inspector Varney that they had been invited to dinner, Holmes had no intention of staying. Accepting Elaina's offer of one of her coaches, he and Watson drove away shortly after the police left. As Elaina and Jesse watched the brougham disappear beyond the trees lining the drive, she asked: 'So what do you think of my friend Holmes now?'

Jesse shrugged. 'He's a hard man to figure out. But I'll give him credit for one thing: he kept his word. He had a chance to hand me over to the law, and he didn't take it.'

Elaina didn't answer. She continued to stare out of the window. Her silence troubled Jesse. 'What's wrong?'

'Nothing.'

'*Something's* wrong,' he insisted. 'What is it? Do you want me to leave? I wouldn't blame you.'

'No, no, that's the last thing I want. It's just that . . . '

'Go on.'

'It's Holmes. I sense you might be right.'

He frowned. 'In what way?'

'That he may not be as trustworthy as I thought.'

Jesse stared at her as if she had gone loco. 'This is one helluva time to tell me.'

'I know. And believe me, Jesse, I'm as shocked as you are to hear myself say that.'

'What made you change your mind?'

'Nothing. I mean, nothing I can exactly point to. It's more like — well, intuition. I just sensed it when you two were arguing over shooting Liggett.'

Jesse didn't say anything.

Elaina, as if overwhelmed by the idea of accusing the venerable Sherlock Holmes of being crafty or deceitful, suddenly blurted: 'Oh, what am I saying? Forget what I just said, Jesse. I must be going crazy to think that Holmes would be anything but totally honest with you.'

Again, Jesse didn't say anything. But the look in his eyes hinted that the seed of suspicion, already lingering there, was now running rampant.

'Maybe what's troubling me,' Elaina continued after a pause, 'is that Holmes has a Machiavellian streak in him.'

'Meaning?'

173

'He'll do anything to get what he wants, to achieve his goal.'

'And what goal might that be, Ellie?'

'I'm not sure yet.'

Jesse grunted. 'And until you are, what the hell am I supposed to do — sit around here waitin' for Mr Two-Face to show his real motive?'

'Being sarcastic won't help,' Elaina chided, adding: 'Oh God, I wish now I hadn't told you what was bothering me. Knowing your temper, you're likely to jump on Duke and go shoot Holmes!'

'That ain't the worst idea you ever had,' Jesse said grimly. Then, as she looked alarmed: 'Don't sweat it. I already promised my brother I wouldn't lose my head if I got into trouble. And I ain't about to go back on my word unless it's truly necessary.'

Elaina sighed, relieved, and put her arms about Jesse's neck. 'I wish Frank was here,' she said softly. 'I'd give him a big kiss for being so smart.'

Jesse grinned, his temper fading. 'Give it to me instead . . . then next time I see him . . . '

Her kiss silenced him.

It was a long, passionate embrace and when their lips finally separated, she pressed her cheek against his chest and closed her eyes.

'I hope you meant what you said before — about trusting me, I mean?'

'How couldn't I?' Jesse said. 'You've stuck your neck out for me, hid me, lied to the police. If that ain't bellyin' up to the bar, I don't know what is.' He cupped his hands about her beautiful face and kissed her uplifted lips.

When they eventually broke apart she took his hand, saying: 'Knowing that makes me happier than I've ever been. Because I've thought of a way to find the Liggetts.'

'Go on.'

'What's the one thing that's better than going after your quarry?' she asked.

He thought for a moment, then shrugged. 'Havin' them come to you?'

'Exactly.'

'Easier said than done.'

She smiled as if knowing a secret. 'Mr James,' she whispered, 'with my plan you can't fail.'

'I'm listenin'.'

'Money,' she said. 'Money, and lots of it.'

'I don't follow.'

'The Liggetts want you out of the way, right? That much is obvious. Well, suppose we offer them a way to get exactly what they want *and* earn themselves a reward in the process?'

It took him a moment to catch on, then he said: 'You mean puttin' a price on my head?'

'Exactly. I can arrange it through my lawyer. The reward will be offered by a concerned citizen who wishes to remain anonymous. And the amount will be large enough to tempt even the Liggetts out into the open.'

'How can you be sure?'

'Because they're the only ones who know that you're here. They must do, or they wouldn't have pretended to be you robbing the bank. And if that doesn't convince you,' she added as he looked doubtful, 'how else did they know where to send the police?'

'I reckon you're right,' Jesse agreed.

'I know I am,' Elaina said. 'Just as I know that when the Liggetts show up to claim the reward, you'll be waiting for them.'

Jesse grinned slowly. 'You ain't just a pretty face, are you?'

'Mr James,' she said softly, 'you don't know the *half* of it.'

He kissed her again, hard and full on the lips. 'Let's go upstairs,' he said.

'In a moment,' she laughed. 'First, I want to show you something.'

★ ★ ★

She led him downstairs to the wine cellar. When she turned up the gaslight he saw that the dank, stone-flagged room was filled with rack upon rack of dusty bottles. 'Although my husband always denied it,' she said, 'his grandfather was said to be involved with smugglers.'

Reaching one particular rack, she reached up and touched something set far back in the shadows and to his surprise the wine rack slowly, silently swung back, revealing a small, shadow-black room.

A candle and a box of phosphor matches sat on a shelf just inside the doorway. She quickly lit the candle and held it high. As the shadows retreated, he saw that the room contained a table upon which sat a large display case, its red velvet shelves sprinkled with everything from brooches and pendants to rings, tiaras, bracelets and necklaces.

'What do you think of my collection?' she asked proudly.

He shook his head in wonder. 'It trumps just about every-thin' — even Abernathy's.'

'Abernathy's?'

'General store in Kearney,' he explained with a self-conscious shrug. 'One day when me'n Frank were young 'uns, Ma took us into town to buy Frank a new shirt. I was real excited, 'cause it meant I'd get his old one.'

'I know that feeling,' she confided, her mood suddenly wistful. 'I wore my sister's hand-me-downs till I was twelve and got to work in Widow Tompkins's dress-shop — ' She caught herself suddenly and said: 'Sorry. I didn't mean to interrupt. Go on.'

'Well, while Ma and Frank were busy, I snuck over to the counter where Mr Abernathy kept all his candy in these big glass jars. I knew Ma didn't have no spendin' money, but I remember looking at them candies and thinking it was the prettiest damn sight I'd ever seen. Till this one.' Again he looked at the jewels. 'Must be worth a fortune.'

'A fortune I'm willing to share with you,' she said. 'On one condition.'

'Who do I have to kill?'

'No killing,' she said. 'Just . . . a favour.'

'Name it.'

'It's taken me years to assemble this collection,' she explained. 'I keep it locked away like this because some of the pieces were acquired in . . . well, let's just say in ways some upstanding folks might frown upon. Now there's only one piece I need to make it complete — a jewel known as the Star of Persia. I'd buy it, but it's in the Royal Museum.'

She turned to face him. 'Steal it for me,

Jesse, and I'll post your reward — one big enough to lure the Liggetts right into your hands.'

He was quiet for a long moment. 'It's a temptin' offer,' he said.

'Is that a yes or a no?'

'First I wanna know somethin',' he said. 'Is that how you got all these jewels? By paying someone to steal 'em for you?'

'Only the pieces I couldn't buy. Does that shock you?'

'I reckon it should,' he replied. 'But it don't.' He gave the proposition another moment's thought before saying: 'This museum. Where is it?'

'West London.'

'I'd need to scout it out first, get to know the lie of the land.'

'That might be risky. Your photograph's already appeared in the afternoon editions. It'll be everywhere by tomorrow.'

'Then we'll just have to take extra care,' he replied. 'Won't we?'

16

Blackrat's Revenge

Although he had been raised in poverty and was poorly educated at best, Blackrat Lynch had learned one particular lesson early in life — that knowledge is power.

It was a concept he'd grasped immediately, for he'd needed both knowledge *and* power to survive the mean streets of East London. Thus, Blackrat had always made a point of keeping his ears open and his mouth shut — well, as shut as his buck teeth would allow — and in that way he picked up a valuable snippet here, a juicy fragment there, and developed an understanding of all the East End's notable comings and goings.

That morning he left his lodgings in Norfolk Street and walked painfully up to the Hand and Dagger public house on Commercial Road. A recent downpour had turned the cobbles slick and oily and everywhere muddy puddles reflected the louring sky.

The minute he entered the pub, which was all but deserted at this early hour, the landlord, Gideon Butterfield, turned to him and said: 'That's funny, seein' you in here.'

Blackrat leaned against the scarred counter and threw down five pennies. 'What's so funny about that?' he demanded belligerently. And then: 'Give me 'alf a pint an' a pig's trotter.'

The landlord busied himself pouring the half-pint first. 'There was a bloke in here, not twenty minutes since, askin' after them Yanks o' yourn.'

Blackrat's expression immediately darkened. He had yet to live down the tale of his beating at the hands of Cage Liggett, and his assorted aches, pains, bruises and swellings were a constant reminder of that humiliation. But his bitterness was quickly replaced by his natural curiosity, that ever-present need to turn knowledge into power.

'What did 'e want, this bloke?' he asked.

Butterfield hooked a steaming trotter out of the crock-pot on the stove and dropped it on to a none-too-clean plate, then passed it across with a knife and fork. 'Wanted to know where to find 'em,' he said.

'Did you tell 'im?'

The landlord gave him a withering look. The answer to that was obvious. He'd never ratted on anyone. You didn't last long in the East End if you did.

'Well, who was 'e, this bloke?' Blackrat persisted. 'Did 'e say why 'e was lookin' for 'em?'

'No,' said the landlord. 'As to who he was, he was just a bloke. About sixty, grey hair, wore a brown cap, an old plaid jacket, grey trousers.'

'Well, good luck to 'im,' Blackrat growled, sipping his drink and then sawing determinedly at the steaming trotter. 'Blokes like them Liggetts, they won't never be found unless they *wants* to be found.'

He took his meal to a corner table and chewed thoughtfully. The door opened and a man named Taffy Craddock came inside. Taffy always stank of mutton fat because he worked at the local candle factory. He bought a drink, joined Blackrat, and for a while the two acquaintances played dominoes and swapped tittle-tattle. At last Taffy left, and soon afterward Blackrat followed suit.

At the combination tobacco shop and barber's on the corner of Plumber's Row he bought an ounce of medium tobacco and some papers. As the assistant took Blackrat's money, he said: 'There was a bloke in 'ere just now, askin' after them two Americans you 'ad that run-in with.'

Not again, thought Blackrat. But he said: 'What did you tell 'im?'

'Nuffink.'

'Which way did 'e go?'

'Down towards Whitechapel. I don't suppose you missed 'im by more than a quarter of an hour.'

Blackrat left the shop and set off for Whitechapel. Again that thought was in his head — that knowledge was power. And knowing why this old feller was trying to find the Liggetts might give him some sort of edge he could use against them.

Although he had to favour his injuries, it didn't take him long to spot the man he was after. He knew his patch well and could spot a stranger a mile off. And the old coot in the well-worn plaid jacket was a stranger, all right. He was just coming out of the copper shop on the other side of Whitechapel Gate when Blackrat spotted him.

Blackrat studied the man. Gideon Butterfield had been right. He was in his sixties and walked with a shuffle that was even more laboured than Blackrat's present limp. He wore a flat cloth cap over his unruly grey hair, and his loose trousers concertinaed comically around his scuffed black boots.

Blackrat watched him shuffle off, shaking his head slightly, maybe in frustration. With elaborate insouciance, he followed him at a discreet distance. When the old man set his left boot up on the edge of a public trough and retied the lace, Blackrat got a closer look at his features. His skin was sallow, his chin whiskery, eyes pouchy and dull. His unwashed grey hair matched his equally unkempt sideburns and mutton-chop moustache.

The old man straightened up and regarded his surroundings. The London Hospital stood on the other side of the busy road, next door to the saw mill. Nearer to hand, a dingy arched passageway led from Whitechapel Road to the clothing manufacturers located along Buck's Row. After another moment's consideration, the old man vanished into the passageway.

Blackrat glanced around, knowing he was never going to get a better chance to have a quiet, unobserved word with the old man. Ignoring the protest of his sore, stiff muscles, he picked up the pace and hurried after him.

The old man was about halfway along the litter-strewn alley when Blackrat caught up with him. The old man heard him splashing through puddles and began to turn. Seconds later Blackrat grabbed him by the shoulder and spun him around, and while the old man was off balance grabbed him by the lapels of his buttoned plaid jacket and rammed him back against the wall. His cap fell off and landed on the damp cobbles.

'Here, what's your game!' cried the old man indignantly.

He made an attempt to break loose, but Blackrat was too strong. He thrust his face forward, his breath reeking of pork and beer.

'You been lookin' for someone,' snarled Blackrat. 'Two someones, actually, a pair o' Yanks, brothers named Liggett — an' I want to know why.'

The old man scowled. 'I dunno what you — '

A newly acquired knife appeared in Blackrat's hand, the tip of the blade drawing blood under his victim's chin. 'Don't deny it, mate! Word gets around . . . an' one way or another it always gets back to me. So — what's your name?'

'Levi Wright,' the old man said reluctantly. And then, defiantly: 'What's it to you?'

'Just want to know the name of the man I'm gonna stick like a pig if 'e don't tell me what I want to know.'

Beneath shaggy brows, Levi Wright's eyes lowered uneasily. He nervously wet his lips, revealing crooked yellow teeth. 'All right,' he said. 'I don't suppose it's no secret. Bloke in the city asked me to nose around, find these Liggetts for him. Gave me a fiver on account and the promise of another when I tell him

185

where he can find 'em.'

'Who was 'e, this feller?'

'I didn't ask his name. Doubt if he would've told me anyway. Said he'd be waitin' outside the Old Broad Street entrance to Liverpool Street station at six every night for the next three nights. I was to meet him there an' let him know how I was gettin' on.'

''Ow come 'e's so interested in the Liggetts?'

'He didn't say an' I didn't ask. But I can tell you this much — he was another Yank. An' I don't think he was plannin' 'em any good. He had this right mean look in his eyes when he described 'em to me. And there was somethin' else about him that give me the willies, as well.'

'What?'

'He was carryin' a brace of pistols. Oh, he didn't know I knew, but I did. When he reached for his wallet, I saw 'em, in holsters, right here.' He gestured to his armpits.

Blackrat felt a chill run through him. There couldn't be that many Yanks in London who went armed and wore shoulder holsters. 'What did 'e look like, this cove?'

'Tall and sturdy. Decent whistle'n toot, some kinda wide-brimmed 'at.'

'An' 'e's lookin' for the Liggetts?'

'Yeah.'

Blackrat scratched his ear, wondering what

to make of it. Only one thing really made sense — that he had about as much love for the Liggetts as the Yank who'd paid this old geezer to find them for him — incredibly, the same bloody Yank who'd stopped them from robbing that countess.

''Ow do I know you ain't just spinnin' a yarn?' he asked.

'I still got the fiver he gave me,' Wright said. Instantly regretting his admission, he tried to leave. But Blackrat grabbed him, demanding: ''And it over.'

'You'd rob an old man?' Wright said defiantly.

'Way I see it, I'm doin' you a favour,' Blackrat said. 'See, I got no love for them Liggetts either, so I'm gonna tell you where your friend with the pistols can find 'em. An' in return, you're gonna give me that fiver you're 'oldin'. That's fair, ain't it? I mean, you'll get another one when you tell 'im where to find 'em.'

'How do I know *you* ain't just spinnin' a yarn?'

'You don't,' said Blackrat. 'Now 'and over that fiver.'

Reluctantly Wright pulled a crisp white five-pound note from his trouser pocket and gave it to Blackrat, who quickly tucked it away.

'All right, 'ere it is,' he said. 'The Liggetts meet up at the Poacher's Pocket, in Cable Street, most nights. You can't miss 'em. They run with a little bloke who's always sniffin', a red-'eaded Irishman and a big mulatto. If they ain't there, then they've got an old barge moored just past the fish market. It's a rickety old rust-bucket, don't look occupied, but it is. I know — I followed 'em back to it the other night. They never even knew I was there.'

Levi Wright digested the information. 'You better not be havin' me on,' he warned.

'I ain't. An' *you* better not tell anyone that you 'eard this from me, got it?'

'Don't worry. I know how to keep a secret.'

'I 'ope so, 'cause you'll be sorry if you don't. Oh, an' when you tell this Yank where to find the Liggetts, ask 'im to put an extra bullet in each of 'em for me. If 'e's the bloke I think he is, 'e'll do it, too.'

He turned and hurried off along the alley without looking back . . . and as Levi Wright watched him go, he underwent a curious transformation. His hunched shoulders slowly straightened, a faint smile chased away his hangdog look, and as he reached up and pulled the false top set of yellow, crooked teeth away from his own, Sherlock Holmes thought: *If that man can*

188

be believed — and in this instance I believe he can — then I have them.

He allowed himself a brief, humourless smile. His presence here today as 'Levi Wright' had served its purpose admirably. Though it had failed to flush the Liggetts themselves from hiding, it had given him what he believed to be solid information as to their whereabouts. All in all, it had been a good morning's work.

He bent and retrieved his cap, then left the alleyway with the old man's shuffle now replaced by his usual brisk, purposeful stride. It was time now to return to Baker Street and decide upon his next course of action. As he doubled back into Whitechapel Road, he knew that no hansom would stop for him in his present sorry state, so he caught the dark-green Bayswater tram instead and found a seat at the back of the vehicle to consider what he had learned.

They run with a little bloke who's always sniffin', a red'eaded Irishman and a big mulatto, his informant had told him. Three men. Three men plus the two Liggett brothers . . . The five men who had robbed Crosbie & Shears? Almost certainly.

It was then, as they passed the corner of Farringdon Street and Ludgate Hill, that

Holmes heard the newspaper boy's cry:

'Read all about it! Daylight robbery at the Royal Museum! Rare gemstone stolen by Jesse James!'

17

The Star of Persia

Some hours earlier . . .

The Royal Museum on Victoria Tower Walk was the very embodiment of British reserve. It stood two storeys tall, with a fussy terracotta façade and high, wide stained-glass windows, and cast a long, spired shadow out across the River Thames, beside which it had been constructed in 1837.

Once through its majestic, varnished-oak doors the atmosphere became musty and studious, for it was a magnificent storehouse filled with all manner of botanical, entomological, mineral and paleontological specimens, fossils, sponges, rare paintings and age-worn sculptures, an exhaustive array of medieval ironwork, arms, armour, enamels, brasswork, pewter . . . and of course precious jewels.

None was more impressive than the Star of Persia.

Presently on loan from the government of Tehran, the Star was said to be one of the original crown jewels plundered by the

Afghans in 1719. Smaller than its better-known counterpart, the Koh-i-Noor, it was nevertheless a spectacular jewel — a fine white diamond of some forty carats that would fit in the palm of an average-sized man's hand.

On the stroke of ten that morning an ancient doorman shuffled to the doors, a ring of thirty keys hanging from one liver-spotted hand. Laboriously he sorted through the keys, one at a time, until he found the one he sought. It would have been quicker to keep the keys separately, of course, but they had always been on this one ring, and sorting through them had become a ritual he had fallen into many years before.

At last he found the key he required and unlocked the doors in his own sweet time.

As the first of the day's visitors began to file inside and fill the building with their shuffling echoes, the old doorman began to hobble back to the staff room below stairs, where he would enjoy a nice cup of tea and a close study of The *Sporting Life* — another of his long-established habits. But even as he started toward the narrow side door that led down to the museum's voluminous basement area, he heard what he took to be the sound of a horse approaching at speed.

He turned, noting that the museum's

visitors had heard the sound too and were now looking back toward the busy street beyond, thinking that perhaps a cabbie was having trouble with his recalcitrant horse.

Instead, they saw a masked man astride a pure white stallion galloping up the wide cement steps toward them.

As people scattered to left and right the horseman surged through the open doors. Keeping the horse at a gallop, he rode across the lobby and beneath a series of terracotta arches toward the central exhibition hall.

At the far end of the hall was a glass case surrounded by an iron cage and a rope barrier. Inside the case, resting on artistically folded red velvet, sat the Star of Persia.

Alerted by the commotion at the front doors and then by the clatter of hoofs on the black-and-white tiled floor, the two elderly guards standing watch over the exhibit hurried forward and defensively raised their hands as if to ward off the rider.

Jesse James knew it would have been easy to run the old boys down, but he admired their courage and drew rein instead.

'Get outta the way, you idiots!' he shouted behind his mask.

The guards dearly wanted to do just that. But they were old soldiers and they still had their pride, so they stood their ground and brandished the short, stout clubs with which they'd been issued.

Jesse cursed and drew one of his Colts.

He fired a couple of shots at the floor between their feet. They leapt into the air and ran for cover, one of them producing a whistle from his pocket and blowing it shrilly.

Ignoring them, Jesse dismounted, grabbed the rope coiled over his saddle horn and quickly knotted it around two of the bars protecting the Star of Persia. He vaulted back into the saddle, wrapped the rope about the pommel and then backed the horse up.

At first nothing happened, except that the stallion, Duke, slipped and left a line of scratches along the polished floor. Jesse urged the creature to greater effort, knowing he didn't have much time. Word of the robbery must have already gone out and the police would soon be converging on the museum from all points of the compass.

As if to prove it, more whistles sounded in every dusty corner of the museum, mingled with the sound of guards racing into the ground-floor exhibition hall. Men were shouting for him to stop, or stay where he was, or lay down his weapon, while others yelled that the police were coming and he'd never get away with it.

Clenching his teeth, Jesse spurred the horse

to greater efforts and this time the two bars started bending outward. 'Come on,' he urged the stallion. 'Come on, dammit, you can do it!'

At last the front section of the cage buckled as it was wrenched out of the floor. Jesse jumped from the saddle, kicked aside the buckled ironwork and smashed the glass display case with the barrel of his Colt.

'Stop him!'

'He's stealing the Star of Persia!'

'Get him!'

'Don't let him get away!'

Jesse heard the commotion — the yells, whistles, the clatter of running men in heavy boots coming ever closer — and ignored all of it. He knew the robbery had taken longer than he'd expected and even as he grabbed the huge diamond, remounted and whirled the stallion around, he saw that the police had already arrived.

Truncheons drawn, they quickly formed a line blocking his path.

Worse, Jesse now spotted another complication he hadn't foreseen — the old goat of a doorman had had the presence of mind to shut the front doors, effectively blocking the outlaw's escape.

Impulsively he reined up, causing the stallion to slide on the marble floor. It almost went down, but somehow kept its balance. Jesse yelled: '*Yaaah!*' and instead of heading for the policemen spurred the horse up the wide, winding staircase to the mezzanine.

Caught off guard by the unexpected move, the policemen immediately broke ranks and charged after him.

The stallion leapt the final few steps, its hoofs clattering on the parquet floor of the circular mezzanine. Jesse loped the horse around the area, glancing into each open door he came to. None offered any escape.

Left with little choice, Jesse guided the stallion through one door and along the length of an enormous room filled with stuffed animals of almost every description, including a separate section devoted to freaks of nature, from albino tigers to cats with two tails.

He headed for the row of stained-glass windows at the far end, reined up and looked through the glass at the street far below. He was rewarded with a vertigo-inducing bird's-eye view of cabs, carts and pedestrians passing in both directions. Realizing that if he jumped he'd be committing suicide, Jesse whirled the horse around.

Policemen now came bursting into the room.

Cursing his luck, Jesse charged them. One

of the policemen threw himself at the horse, grabbed the back of Jesse's jacket and almost tore him from the saddle. He used the truncheon in his free hand to strike Jesse in the back. Hurt, Jesse twisted and aimed his revolver at the man, saw that he was young and scared, and knew he couldn't pull the trigger.

Instead he spun the horse around, the sudden unexpected manoeuvre breaking the policeman's hold. He went flying, crashing into a display case that toppled over and hit a stuffed bear exhibit. The huge grizzly teetered for a prolonged moment, then fell forward, pinning the howling constable underneath it.

By now still more policemen were blocking the doorway. Jesse drew his Colt and fired over their heads. Two bullets punched holes into the plaster above the lintel and the policemen scattered. Desperate, Jesse spurred the stallion forward and the big white horse galloped back out into the mezzanine.

The constables and museum staff raced after them.

Jesse spurred the stallion onward and entered a room on the other side of the mezzanine. It was filled with fossils of all shapes and sizes, presented in a bewildering maze of display cases. For an instant the stallion broke stride, not sure where to go, and reared up, neighing shrilly. At once Jesse brought his fist down between the horse's flattened ears. It dropped back on to all fours, and then took off between the rows of display cases filled with rocks and fossils. Jesse guided the horse down the nearest aisle. At the end of it was a wall in which stood a row of large windows.

'We've got him now!' yelled one of the constables.

'He won't get away this time!' shouted another.

Jesse twisted in the saddle, and fired a bullet over their heads. Police and staff immediately took cover, giving Jesse time to look quickly through the window at the Thames below.

Far, *far* below.

Tugs and barges plied her grimy waters, but those same waters promised a marginally softer landing than the cobbles of Victoria Tower Walk on the other side of the museum.

As if sensing its rider's intention, the stallion snorted, stamped and shook its head, mane flying. Forcing the animal to back up, Jesse growled: 'I'm warnin' you, you son of a lop-eared mule. Either you jump or I'll make you eat the evidence! Your call.'

Duke hesitated, as if considering the alternative.

Then man and beast seemed to reach a mutual decision, and Jesse yelled: 'Aw, hell, hoss, let's do it!'

He whirled the stallion away from the window and rode back to the opposite wall. Then, with teeth clenched, he turned the horse again and spurred its flanks. Duke surged forward, hoofs clattering on the floor.

The multicoloured window rushed towards them.

Jesse gave a wild shout and clung to the reins.

The window loomed up directly in front of them. Fearing that the stallion might balk at the last instant, Jesse dug his spurs into its flanks.

The stallion surged forward and without any hesitation leapt through the glass.

The window exploded outwards with a thunderous crash. It was followed by a weird, disorienting moment of absolute silence as man and horse sailed through the air, shards of glass spinning and tumbling around them.

Then —

Jesse felt the wind pulling him backwards out of the saddle. He let the reins go, felt them lashing his arms and shoulders like whips — and doggedly clung to the saddle horn with both hands.

Beneath him the horse's legs kept pumping, as if he were trying to run on air.

Jesse looked down and saw their momentum had carried them beyond the narrow footpath below, out over the water . . .

As they plunged downward, the horse gave a scream that was so womanlike Jesse wondered if his ears had betrayed him. Still clinging to the saddle horn, he followed the stallion down, his own legs pumping wildly as the Thames rushed nearer, nearer, nearer . . .

Man and horse hit the water with an ear-shattering explosion. Cold water burst up around them in a great spray. An instant later they sank beneath the surface.

The impact pounded the wind out of Jesse, jamming his sodden bandanna into his mouth. He gagged, unable to breathe, and panicked.

The stallion recovered first. Submitting to instinct, it began to fight its way back to the sun-dappled surface, leaving Jesse to hang on and hope they would make it before his lungs burst.

It took much, much longer than he expected and there was a moment when he thought he wasn't going to survive.

But finally they both broke the surface, Jesse, hatless now, his bandanna swept away, gasping and laughing, choking and spitting foul water all at the same time.

He heard yelling. Looking up, he saw faces filling the shattered window and knew he couldn't rest yet — he and the stallion still had to get out of there.

He groped around in the water until he found the trailing reins, then started swimming toward a set of moss-covered stone steps leading up to the footpath.

The stallion obeyed the tug of the reins and started swimming alongside him.

They reached the steps together. Jesse scrambled out of the water first, dripping and shivering, followed by the stallion. The big white horse shook itself like a dog, spraying droplets everywhere. Exhausted, Jesse was wearily preparing to mount up when he heard yelling behind him.

'There! There he is! Get him!'

He turned just in time to see three policemen from the Bow Street Horse Patrol galloping around the corner of the museum astride big, heavy hunters. As soon as they saw him they blew their whistles and yelled for him to stop, that he was under arrest.

Jesse thought: *To hell with that!*

Quickly mounting, he gave the stallion another dose of the spurs. The horse leapt forward and thundered in the opposite direction. Jesse took the first left — a narrow, cobbled alley leading back toward Victoria Tower Walk. At the far end he burst out on to the thoroughfare with barely any warning, scattering pedestrians and scarcely missing all the horse-drawn traffic. He crossed the street with angry yells ringing in his ears and sent the stallion down another, less busy alleyway. Ahead, behind a row of black iron railings, he saw a park — a sign identified it as Victoria Tower Gardens, a great sward of grass and trees that provided a buffer between the Royal Museum and its near neighbour, the Palace of Westminster. He galloped through the gates and headed for the wooded area.

By the time the police reached the park, there was no sign of the man who'd stolen the Star of Persia.

18

Prelude to a Showdown

As soon as Holmes arrived back at Baker Street Watson leapt up from his chair.

'Have you heard the news?' he demanded. 'I can't believe that James would do something so . . . so . . . irresponsible! The man is here for revenge, not to embark upon a new career as a jewel thief!'

'Quite so,' said Holmes, removing his cap and wig.

'So what do we do about it? Confront him? It'll be dangerous, Holmes. The man is a known killer.'

'A confrontation with Mr James will have to wait,' said Holmes. 'We have other matters to attend to first.'

He vanished into his room, where he remained just long enough to remove all trace of 'Levi Wright' from his person. When he reappeared he was dressed in a black Prince Albert, and together he and Watson travelled by hansom to the Royal Museum.

Following the robbery the museum had

been closed for the day. But they were allowed in when Holmes introduced himself to the flustered curator, Professor Stanley Longford.

There were signs of chaos everywhere. In particular Holmes was drawn to the marks the robber's horse had left in the wooden floor of the mezzanine. He knelt and studied them for several minutes before moving on.

Since the robbery had been committed within the confines of the Metropolitan Police Force's Whitehall Division, it had fallen to Inspector Maxwell Byron to investigate the crime. Holmes and Watson found him peering out through the shattered window at the grey Thames below, while his men continued to scour both floors for clues.

'Confound the man!' said Byron, after he'd shaken hands with them. 'Whoever he is.'

'You don't believe it is Jesse James, then?'

'No, sir, I do not. And for three very good reasons. One, there's nothing to indicate that Jesse James is even in the country. Two, he's a bank or train robber. He deals in hard cash. This kind of crime isn't him at all.' He shook his head. 'No, sir. And thirdly — Fleet Street has simply linked James's name to the crime because it will sell more papers. But may I ask your interest in the matter, Mr Holmes?'

'I am intrigued by the audacity of the

crime,' Holmes replied vaguely.

Unconvinced, Byron studied him shrewdly. He was a tall, remarkably good-looking man, and as tenacious as a starving rat. 'I know you are a man of integrity, Mr Holmes, so I have to take you at your word. But I am aware that you have been helping Rosier of T Division with the recent spate of jewellery thefts. And of course you were quick to visit Inspector Varney of the City of London Police following the Crosbie and Shears robbery.'

Holmes smiled. He had always liked Byron, who was quick and imaginative.

'But there,' Byron continued, 'I fear the similarity ends.'

'Why do you say that?' Watson asked.

'Because the robbery of a country house and the robbery of a city bank pale by comparison with this. As I'm sure you can imagine, this is very likely to cause a serious diplomatic incident if that stone isn't returned.'

Watson looked at the jagged remains of the window and shook his head. 'Hard to believe someone could actually jump a horse out of a window into the river and live to talk about it.'

'But from that feat we can deduce that the thief was a man of great nerve and has no small talent as a rider,' said Holmes. 'He is also used to thinking on his feet. He almost certainly visited the museum sometime within the past day or two to get the lie of the land and formulate his plan, but when it went wrong and the doors were closed, preventing him from making his getaway, he quickly found another means of escape. If you haven't already done so, Inspector, I suggest you ask your men to question the museum staff to see if they remember anyone paying particular attention to the Star of Persia.'

'I have already done that, sir.'

Holmes himself glanced through the shattered window. 'You say the police lost him in the woods on the other side of the park?' he asked.

'Yes, Mr Holmes. But by all accounts it wasn't much of a chase. To hear them tell it, they felt they might just as well have been chasing winged Pegasus, the way that horse flew away from them.'

'That does not surprise me,' Holmes remarked. 'No ordinary horse could have made that leap into the river. Well,' he added briskly, 'we cannot tarry overlong, Inspector. We too have work to do.'

'Of course, sir. But, ah, before you go . . . '

'Yes?'

'Is there anything else you can tell me that might be of use? We really *do* need to find this jewel quickly, you know.'

Holmes considered briefly, then said: 'You are looking for a recently shoed horse of between sixteen and seventeen hands, whose skills would normally be employed in show jumping or perhaps dressage.'

'How can you possibly know that?' asked Byron, frowning.

'The marks your thief's horse left on the floor outside show a stride of approximately twelve feet, or one stride for every four taken by an average man. Size that up accordingly and you get an impressive horse indeed. As near as I can tell, the scuffs show little or no wear — hence, the animal was shoed recently, perhaps in preparation for this very crime. In addition, the shoes were fitted with caulkins.'

'Caulkins?'

'They're cleats, more or less,' said Watson. ''Frost studs' if you like. They're brazed or screwed to the shoe to improve the creature's balance and give it greater traction. Your own police mounts wear them, I believe.'

Holmes smiled. 'Well done, Watson. Oh, and by the way, Inspector. You have one of the animal's mane-hairs stuck to your sleeve.'

Byron looked down, saw the offending hair and quickly peeled it off. 'A *mane*-hair, eh?' he asked, raising one eyebrow.

Holmes nodded. 'Certainly. A hair from its

207

tail would have been noticeably longer and considerably less flexible. Good day, Byron.'

* * *

In his room at Montague Hall Jesse climbed out of the tub and towelled himself dry. The hot bath had chased away the last of his chills and he felt as close to contentment as he had since this whole thing had started.

It had taken him a long time to make it safely back to the house. Not only was he still largely unfamiliar with the city, he had also felt it prudent to double back on himself several times just in case he was being followed. It was almost two o'clock when Elaina's residence eventually came into sight and he heaved a sigh of relief.

He didn't enter by the front, but followed the river-facing wall at the back of the gardens. The wall was high and covered with ivy. Had it not been for one particular tree-stump he could never have found the hidden gate by which he had left early that same morning.

He dismounted, rummaged among the ivy for a few moments, eventually found the gate, then pulled a key from his still-sodden pocket. He unlocked the gate, pushed it open and drove the stallion through with a slap on the rump. He relocked the gate, rearranged the ivy to disguise the portal and dragged himself up and over the wall. He then wearily stepped back into the saddle and rode Duke to the stables.

⋆ ⋆ ⋆

Elaina was waiting for him in the library. When at last he entered, soaked and with soggy boots squelching, she gasped at his condition and demanded to know what happened.

'Nothin' you need worry about,' he said, grinning. Bringing his hand from behind him, he held up the Star of Persia between forefinger and thumb.

The sight took her breath away.

She rushed to him and grabbed the large, flawless diamond. 'Oh my God,' she breathed. 'It's even more beautiful than I remember!'

Jesse watched as she went to the window and admired the jewel, lovingly turning it over and over so that it sparkled in the sunlight.

'This is *it*, Jesse, the last piece I need for my collection. Now it's complete. *I'm* complete.' She smiled and closed her eyes. 'I wish I were a poet, so I could truly describe how I feel.'

'You're doin' fine,' Jesse said. He shivered,

adding: 'If it's OK with you, Ellie, I'll head upstairs and take a hot bath. Get rid of these chills.'

'Good idea.' She reached up on tiptoe and kissed him. 'But hurry back, darling. I want to share my joy with you.'

Now, warm and clean, he tossed the towel aside and dressed in fresh clothes. Outside, the afternoon was sliding toward dusk and sunset was painting the grounds in sweeping shades of amber and pumpkin orange.

He went downstairs and found Elaina in the sitting room. There was no sign of the Star. 'Gotten tired of it already, have you?' he teased.

'I'll never get tired of it,' she said, 'or you.' Rising, she pressed against him. 'You've made me the happiest woman alive.'

'Happy enough to still stump up that reward money?'

'Shame on you, Jesse James. I know you're joking, but to even *think* I would renege . . . ' She crossed to a portrait of Rupert Montague that hung beside the fireplace and unhooked it to reveal a small wall safe.

Behind her, Jesse went to the drinks trolley and poured himself two fingers of Scotch. As he did so he watched her reflection in the circular mirror in front of him. She spun the combination back and forth, then opened the safe and reached inside.

As her hand closed around the pearl-handled, nickel-plated, two-shot derringer it contained, her eyes hardened. 'Maybe this will put an end to your suspicions,' she said over her shoulder.

But before she could turn back to him, they heard the jangle of the front-door bell. Elaina quickly returned the derringer to the safe and locked it.

Jesse peered out the window. 'You expectin' anyone?'

'No.'

'Then go see who it is an' stall 'em, if you can. I'll cover the safe.' He took the portrait from her and as she left he carefully replaced it on the wall. He then unbuttoned his coat so he could easily reach for his Colts, wondering as he did whether he could have slipped up somehow and led the police right to her door.

A few moments later, Elaina returned with Holmes and Watson in tow.

'Forgive us for intruding, Countess,' Holmes said. Then to Jesse: 'May I assume that you have heard the news?'

'What news?' interrupted Elaina.

'Your Mr Liggett has struck again,' said Holmes. 'He robbed the Royal Museum this morning and rode off in broad daylight with the Star of Persia.'

'My God,' Elaina gasped. 'How terrible!'

'How terrible indeed,' Holmes agreed. 'Relations are already strained enough as it is with Tehran. They may turn even uglier if we cannot return it in a timely fashion. Of course,' he added, 'if we are lucky, it may not come to that.'

Elaina said: 'You mean you've found the Liggetts?'

'I believe so. As soon as we leave here, Watson and I are going to confront them.'

'Count me in,' Jesse said grimly.

'I believe we have already discussed that, Mr James,' Holmes said sternly. 'They will pay for their crimes, on that I give you my oath. But I will not stand by and watch you murder them in cold blood.'

'An' if they try to shoot me first?'

'I can condemn no man for acting in defence of himself.'

'Then that's the way we'll play it,' said Jesse. 'For now, anyway.'

Worried, Elaina said: 'Jesse, you can't go. The streets will be teeming with policemen in the wake of the robbery . . . '

'I'm afraid she's right,' said Holmes. 'And I should tell you that your enemies have been far from idle in the interim, Mr James. They have already covered the East End of London in wanted posters, and the likeness they have used is remarkably accurate.'

'That's a chance I'll have to take,' Jesse said. ''Sides, it'll be dark soon.'

'Maybe,' said Elaina. 'But it's still an unnecessary risk. Remember,' she went on, 'once we post that reward, Liggett will play right into your hands.'

'What reward?' Holmes asked quickly.

Ignoring him, Jesse said: 'It could be days, maybe weeks before Liggett takes the bait. This is *now*, and I like my chances.'

'Well, at least show a little sense and take my brougham,' she begged. 'I doubt the police will stop you if you're riding in a coach that bears the Montague arms.'

'Splendid idea,' Holmes said. 'Thank you, Countess. We will dismiss our own waiting hansom and do as you suggest.'

19

Fresh Out of Brothers

Just before he joined the others in Elaina's brougham, Holmes gave their destination to the driver: 'The Pool of London. A public house called The Poacher's Pocket, in Cable Street.'

'Yes, sir,' said Prescott.

As Holmes closed the door behind him and sat beside Watson Jesse made his move. He whipped out one of his pistols and aimed it at Holmes. Watson's eyes opened wide in surprise and he reached for his own service revolver.

'Stay your hand, Watson,' Holmes said quickly. 'There is no need for violence. Mr James suspects I'm leading him into a trap.'

'Ain't you?' asked Jesse, adding: 'You can quit your play-actin', Holmes. We've been on to you for some time now.'

Holmes arched an eyebrow. ' "We?" ' Ah, yes, that would be the countess, of course. What did she tell you? That I couldn't be trusted? That I was really working with the police to bring you to justice?' In the dark of the cab his lips thinned. 'I think it is time we laid our cards on the table, Mr James — beginning with the countess.'

'What about her?' Jesse asked warily.

'I am afraid she has been using you. Perhaps not from the very first, but certainly since she discovered who you really were.'

'What're you talkin' about?'

'The Star of Persia — didn't you steal it for her this very morning?'

'You know I didn't,' Jesse said calmly. 'Hell, you said yourself that it was Liggett.'

'That was strictly for the countess's benefit.'

'Meaning?'

'I do not want her to know that I am on to her little game just yet.' He leaned forward, closer to Jesse. 'Now admit it: Elaina asked you to steal the Star of Persia for her, didn't she? Just as she has engaged others, through one agent or another, to steal for her in the past.'

'You got some steak to back up that sizzle?'

'I have been investigating the countess for some time now. Has she told you anything of her past?'

'She told me her pa ran a hotel in Kansas City,' Jesse said grudgingly. 'That's where she met her husband, that Earl feller.'

'Well, it is certainly true that she was born in Kansas City. However, she was employed as a dancehall girl at the Empress Saloon when she first met the Earl. Her real name is Ellie Corbin. She was born into great poverty but with incurably expensive tastes. She deliberately set out to beguile Earl Montague and marry him as a means of inheriting his fortune.'

'That's a lie!'

'I wish it were, Mr James, for it gives me no pleasure to speak thus. The truth is that within months of their return from the United States, the earl met with an unfortunate accident. According to the countess, who was the only witness, he was descending a staircase when he misjudged a step and fell, breaking his neck. The countess was apparently heartbroken, but her lawyer, Sir Ashley Danvers-Cole, suspected that all was not as it appeared. Upon his own examination of the body he discovered that the earl's injuries were more consistent with a fall *backwards*, not forwards, as the countess had testified. A further, more thorough examination of the earl's chest revealed five small bruises upon each of his shoulders, which were consistent with the tips of four fingers and one thumb, pushing against the flesh. They were almost gone by the time he inspected the body, and would ordinarily not have shown at all, except that the earl suffered from inflammation of the blood vessels — which gives rise to easy bruising.'

'So why didn't this lawyer feller have her arrested?'

'Because the evidence was circumstantial at best, and open to interpretation,' said Holmes. 'However, because it chafed him that she should get away with the murder of a decent and honourable man, he engaged me to keep an eye on her and wait for her to make a mistake.

'I did not have to wait long,' he continued. 'It quickly became clear that the acquisition of wealth and beauty is an obsession with the countess. She is of headstrong and deter-mined disposition, and she will acquire whatever she desires by any means necessary — including treachery.'

'You sayin' she's got a Machiavellian streak?' Jesse said, recalling how Elaina had described Holmes.

Holmes gave him a quizzical look, as if surprised that someone of his background would use such a term. 'In a manner of speaking, yes,' he said then. 'Have you seen her collection, I wonder? I cannot list every jewel of course, for much of it has been purchased legitimately. But among her more recent and questionable acquisitions are a rare and distinctive pair of teardrop earrings, a gold diamond pendant, a pearl bracelet and a three-string mourning necklace in jet, onyx and jasper. I am not an expert in such matters, but I imagine the Star of Persia sits rather well with them.'

Jesse eyed Holmes uneasily. 'If this is more of your fancy 'deducing', I ain't fallin' for it.'

'You still don't trust me?' And then, when Jesse didn't answer: 'Very well. If you won't trust me, sir, you will just have to shoot me.'

'Holmes!' breathed Watson.

Holmes braced himself. Jesse appeared to be just a heartbeat away from pulling the trigger. But something about Holmes's direct, confident stare made the man from Missouri hesitate.

Holmes smiled fleetingly. 'Indecision is not something I expected from you, Mr James.'

'Let's just say I like to get all my ducks in a row 'fore I blow a feller's head off,' Jesse growled. 'But let's get one thing straight — just 'cause I'm givin' you the benefit of the doubt, don't think I won't shoot you if . . . '
He paused as the coach began slowing down, and glanced out of the window. 'We here?' he asked.

Holmes peered out into the near-darkness. 'Yes.'

Jesse gave Holmes one last long, hard look and then holstered his Colt. 'Let's go.'

Prescott had parked the coach on the opposite side of the road to the pub. The trio climbed out and studied their surroundings. The night was quiet and a sulphurous mist was drifting in off the Thames. Here and there lights twinkled aboard some of the boats at anchor. Suddenly a burst of laughter drifted to them from the pub across the street, and they looked at each other.

'Remember our agreement, Mr James,' said Holmes. 'You may do as you will, in self-defence. But I will not be a party to cold-blooded murder.'

Jesse's only response was a grunt that could have meant anything. He then started across the road toward the pub, Holmes and Watson following.

Inside, business was brisk and customers had to shout to be heard above the noise. A drifting pall of cigarette and pipe smoke hung like a shroud over everything. Holmes had to squint in order to perceive their quarry, hunched conspiratorially around a table in the corner. Except for the numbers — there were only three men instead of the five he had been expecting — it was exactly as his informant had told him; a young, dark-haired man was in the company of a large mulatto and a redhead.

'Unless I am mistaken,' Holmes said to Jesse, 'that would be Jack Liggett?'

Jesse nodded, his ice-blue eyes hooding dangerously. 'An' them other two, they're part of the gang that tried to rob Ellie.'

He started forward, only stopping when Watson pressed the barrel of his Webley against Jesse's spine. 'Let's not be hasty, Mr James,' he said through clenched teeth.

Jesse looked back at him disdainfully. 'You ain't no back-shooter, Watson.'

'Of course not. But I fancy the prospect of a bullet in the leg or the shoulder will make you think twice before you do anything rash.'

Jesse ignored the warning and strode purposefully through the crowd.

When he reached the corner table, he halted and said quietly: 'Sorry to interrupt, boys, but what am I robbin' next?'

Startled, all three looked up. They paled as they recognized Jesse.

He pulled back his coat to reveal his holstered pistols, adding: 'Another bank, maybe?'

For an instant Jack Liggett's nerve broke altogether. Then he recovered himself and tried to hide his fear behind a mocking sneer. 'Well, if it ain't the great Jesse James himself!

What're you gonna do now, James — gun us down in cold blood? This ain't Missoura, y'know. We're not armed.'

'Neither were Ma an' Doc Samuel an' little Archie — but that didn't stop you or your murderin' brother from tryin' to kill 'em.'

'That was a mistake an' you know it . . . ' began Jack.

He broke off, alarmed, as Jesse drew his pistols.

'Then I reckon one mistake deserves another,' Jesse said, and his fingers tightened around the triggers.

'If you shoot him,' a voice said calmly behind Jesse, 'we might never find out where his brother is hiding.'

Jesse glanced over his shoulder and saw Holmes and Watson regarding him gravely. Jesse turned back to Jack Liggett, the urge to kill him almost impossible to control. Grudgingly holstering his pistols, Jesse leaned close to the younger Liggett and said: 'You want to live — tell us where your brother's holed up?'

'I don't *have* a brother,' Jack said.

'Don't insult us by lying,' said Watson.

'I ain't lyin'.' Jack turned to his companions: 'Do I have a brother?'

They solemnly shook their heads.

'Sorry,' Jack said flippantly. 'Fresh out of brothers.'

Jesse whipped out one of his Colts and fired.

Jack screamed and clutched his right hand, blood squirting from between his fingers. 'You bastard!' he wailed, cradling his injured hand to his chest.

Watson blanched, murmured: 'Good Lord . . . '

Everyone in the pub fell silent. Seeing Jesse's gun and Liggett's bloody hand, they quickly shuffled back to give the group gathered about the corner table plenty of space.

Meanwhile, Jack examined his bleeding hand and realized that the tip of his little finger was missing, leaving only a ragged, bloody stump. *'Goddamn* you!' he hissed at Jesse. 'Only a gutless yellow belly would shoot an unarmed man!'

Jesse quickly drew his other Colt and placed the gun on the table before Jack. 'Pick it up,' he said.

'An' have you shoot me 'fore I can grab it — no thanks.'

Jesse holstered his remaining Colt and stepped back. 'How about *now*?' he said. 'Or ain't you got the sand for a fair fight?'

Jack went white but didn't answer.

'Figures,' Jesse mocked when Jack didn't move. 'You'n your brother are mighty brave when it comes to maiming women and killin' young 'uns . . . but facin' someone who's gonna shoot back . . . that's a mule of a different colour, ain't it?'

Jack nervously wet his lips. 'You're just lookin' for an excuse to kill me,' he said. 'An' I'm not gonna give it to you.'

Jesse smiled, a cruel dangerous smile that froze Jack's blood.

'This ain't about me,' he said, drawing his Colt again. 'It's about what you'n Cage done to my family. So either you tell me where your brother's hidin' or the next shot's gonna clip off an ear, Jack.'

He thumbed back the hammer.

'N-No!' Jack begged. 'No . . . don't . . . don't do that. Put up your damn . . . iron.'

'Tell me where Cage is and I will,' Jesse said.

'I c-can't! I mean, it's too late! My brother lit out! He heard you was after him an' . . . an' he went north . . . said he'd write me when he found someplace . . . to stay.'

'You're lyin'!' snarled Jesse.

'I swear it!'

Jesse aimed his Colt at Jack's right ear.

'D-Don't . . . Please, don't. I . . . '

He stopped as someone entered the pub and Jesse saw recognition cross his face as he identified the newcomer.

Thinking it might be Jack's brother, Jesse whirled, ready to shoot — but instead saw a small, rat-faced man whose nose was running. Recognizing Jesse, Alfie Adams quickly started to leave.

Jesse snapped off a shot, the bullet punching into the heavy wooden door close to Alfie's head. Yelping with fear, Alfie turned and fled from the pub.

Jesse grabbed Jack, dragged him to his feet and jammed the barrel of his six-gun against his temple. 'Talk straight, damn you, or I'll blow a hole through you.'

Watson started to protest but Holmes silenced him with a brusque gesture.

Jack hesitated, eyes popping with fear. Jesse thumbed back the hammer and at last Jack broke. 'All right, all right,' he whined. 'I'll tell you.'

'You'll do better than that,' snarled Jesse. 'You'll take us to him yourself. And remember this, Jack: if that little weasel's gone to warn Cage and he fixes to bushwhack us, you'll be right there to take the first bullet.'

20

A Death in the Family

Alfie ran all the way to the barge. There, exhausted, he staggered aboard and joined Cage Liggett under the tattered awning, where he gasped out what he'd seen at the Poacher's Pocket. 'It was 'im, guv'! I swear on me mum's grave. Same Yank wiv the guns who stopped us from robbin' the countess's coach. Only this time, there was two toffs wiv 'im.'

Liggett chewed anxiously on his lip. 'What'd they look like?'

'One was tall an' thin an' the other, 'e carried a stick.'

Liggett frowned, not recognizing the descriptions. 'Go on,' he said.

'The Yank, 'e shot your brother, Cage! I 'eard the bang just as I was enterin' the pub, but didn't realize what it was 'til I saw 'im standin' there with a ruddy great pistol in 'is 'and!'

Liggett swallowed hard. 'He killed Jack?'

'Nah, nah, just wounded 'im, looked like. I

turned tail and scarpered just before 'e took a shot at me, too!'

'Did they follow you?'

'Nah. 'Least, I don't think so. But you never know. Could be I just didn't see 'em in all this fog.' He sniffed and wiped his nose on his sleeve, adding: 'They come in a coach.'

'How do you know?'

''Cause I saw it waitin' 'cross the road. Same coach me'n my mates tried to rob the night you took over from Blackrat. I recognized the crest on the door.'

Liggett looked out into the swirling fog. So Jesse had tracked him down after all, he thought grimly. Well, so be it. At least he had the jump on him. On top of that there was the fog. With any luck, he could use it to set a trap for Jesse . . . shoot him from behind before the outlaw even had a chance to draw.

'Wait here for me,' he told Alfie.

'Wot, an' get shot? Not bleedin' likely.'

Liggett grabbed him and lifted him up till only his toes touched the deck. 'Would you sooner I filled your pockets with rocks an' dumped you in the goddamn river?'

'Awright, awright,' Alfie said, squirming. 'I'll wait. 'Onest.'

'And keep your eyes peeled. Let me know if you hear or see that coach coming.' Liggett ducked down the steps into the cabin before

226

Alfie could protest.

When he returned a few minutes later he had a Navy Colt tucked in his waistband and carried two unlit oil lamps.

'Here's what we're gonna do,' he said, thrusting one of the lamps at Alfie.

''Mean you're gonna make a fight of it?'

'What choice do I have?' Liggett asked. 'I've already come six thousand miles an' Jesse found me. No,' he added grimly, 'we're gonna settle this now, once an' for all. C'mon.'

He led the frightened little man ashore. Once on the dock, each took up his position, Alfie in a recessed warehouse doorway on the other side of the narrow lane, Liggett behind a stack of empty barrels awaiting collection by the local drayman. All that was left to them then was the hardest job of all — the waiting game.

The minutes dragged by. Nerves stretched taut, Liggett jumped at every stray sound that drifted to him on the damp musty-smelling air.

Suddenly he stiffened. Through the fog he could hear the sound of approaching horses, the rattle of wheels on slick cobbles. He suddenly remembered the lamp in his hand and what it was for. He dug out a match and struck it on a barrel. The match spluttered and died. He fumbled out another. This time the match flared to life. He quickly lit the lamp.

The coach drew closer. Peering between the barrels, he saw it as a vague, dark block gradually growing larger through the mist.

Mouth dry, he waited for it to come closer, pumping himself up for what had to be done. This was kill or be killed. It was the chance to stop living with one eye forever on his shoulder, to get back at Jesse for shooting Jack.

The coach came out of the night, mist swirling around the trotting horses. As it drew level with him Liggett jumped up and hurled the lamp in through the open side window. There was a loud smash of glass, followed by a *whoomf*! as the oil ignited.

Almost simultaneously Alfie, hidden on the other side of the road, threw his lamp as well. It burst aflame inside the coach and suddenly the elegant brougham was an inferno on wheels.

The panicked horses broke into a mad gallop, each one showing the whites of its eyes as it looked back and then tried to outrun the conflagration that was chasing them.

Liggett broke cover. Sprinting alongside the coach, he emptied his Colt into the flaming brougham. The panicked horses screamed louder and ran faster. They tried to take the corner at the end of the street with the burning coach still rocking wildly behind them, sending shadows leaping high across the warehouse walls, but they were going too fast. The blazing coach leaned over on to two wheels and finally crashed on to its side, sparks showering skyward. There followed a loud splintering as the tongue was ripped away from the running gear, then the horses, free at last of their fiery burden, raced off into the fog.

Winded, Liggett excitedly ran up to the burning coach. He tried to look inside, hoping to see Jesse and his friends in flames, but the heat was too much and he had to keep his distance. Alfie hurried up beside him, shouting breathlessly: 'Nice work, guv!'

They stood there, watching the fire, flames hot on their faces, Liggett gleefully enjoying the moment. He could hardly believe that, in the end, it had all been so easy. There was only one thing that bothered him.

'Where's the coachman?' he asked.

'Eh?'

'I didn't see any driver,' Liggett said. 'There was no one *drivin'* this thing!'

'Maybe 'e fell off,' suggested Alfie. 'Or jumped off when the fire started.'

'Don't worry about the coachman,' a voice said behind them. 'We told him to make himself scarce before we sent the coach on ahead of us.'

Liggett and Alfie spun round in time to see Jesse stride purposefully out of the fog, with Holmes and Watson alongside him. Watson was prodding Jack Liggett ahead of him with his service revolver.

'Bugger be'old!' Alfie said. 'We've been 'ad, guv'.'

'You have indeed, gentlemen,' confirmed Holmes.

Liggett glared at Jesse. It was an odd moment. He felt he knew the outlaw so well, and yet this was the first time they'd ever come face to face. He cursed and brought his gun up to shoot Jesse — then remembered he'd emptied it into the coach.

He went cold, but to his credit he didn't whine. 'Go ahead,' he said flatly. 'Shoot me. Get it over with.'

'Don't tempt me,' said Jesse.

'Gentlemen,' said Holmes, 'you may consider yourselves seized and detained until the police arrive, at which time you will be taken before a justice of the peace, who shall proceed with all convenient dispatch to the hearing and determining of the complaint against you — in your case, Mr Liggett, that will mean deportation back to the United States, where you will answer to the attempted murder of Zerelda Samuel in Missouri, and the actual murder of her son, Archie.'

'The hell you say!'

Liggett threw his empty gun at Jesse.

The man from Missouri dodged the weapon, but it had already served its purpose — to distract him and give Liggett the split second he needed to make his move. He hurled himself at Jesse, his weight and momentum sending them both sprawling.

At the same time Jack elbowed Watson in the belly and then, heedless of the pain in his wounded hand, jumped him. Both slammed to the ground, grappling for Watson's revolver.

Alfie, seeing his chance, whipped out a rusty cargo-hook and flung himself at Holmes.

He had no way of knowing that Holmes was a master of *baritsu*, the Japanese art of wrestling, until Holmes blocked the blow, crowded him, spun around, grabbed Alfie's belt and then leaned forward, throwing him neatly from the hip.

Alfie landed hard and the cargo-hook slid away from him. As he started after it, Holmes leapt forward and blocked his path. Alfie hesitated, then again attacked him. This time Holmes used his forearm to block the blow, and struck out with a blindingly fast ridge-hand blow that hit the main artery in Alfie's neck. Rendered helpless and almost insensible, Alfie felt Holmes slam against his left shoulder. He staggered back, giving Holmes time to hook one leg behind Alfie's feet and sweep the little criminal's legs out from under him.

Jesse, meanwhile, threw Liggett off him and scrambled to his feet. Liggett rose too, and both men circled, each looking for an opening. Liggett suddenly charged Jesse, swinging wildly. Jesse sidestepped, and clasping his hands together slammed Liggett to the ground. The ex-Pinkerton operative was up almost immediately, this time lunging for one of Jesse's Colts. He managed to jerk one from its holster and, stepping back, brought the gun up to fire.

Then he heard someone coming up behind him. Fearing it was one of Jesse's friends, Liggett whirled and fired.

Too late he saw it was his brother, who'd knocked Watson off his feet and was hurrying to help Liggett finish Jesse.

Jack stopped, doubling over as the .45 slug buried itself in his belly. Eyes wide, mouth slack, he stared at Cage as if he couldn't believe what had happened.

His disbelief was mirrored in Liggett's own look of horror. 'Jack?'

Jack worked his frothing lips but no sound came out. He pitched forward and was dead before he hit the ground.

Distraught, Liggett started toward his brother; then, remembering Jesse, he whirled and went to shoot him. Before he could pull the trigger Holmes kicked the gun from his hand. When Jesse pulled his other Colt Liggett lost his nerve and ran off into the fog.

'Damn you, Holmes!' snapped Jesse, trying to get a clear bead on Liggett before the fog swallowed him up altogether. 'Get the hell out of my way!'

But it was already too late. All that remained of Liggett now was the sound of his fading footsteps.

Holmes, meanwhile, was already joining Watson at Jack's side. Watson looked up as he approached and shook his head, indicating that Jack was beyond medical aid.

Jesse joined them and glanced down at the body. 'One down,' he said grimly, 'one to go.'

'We'll take him alive, if we can,' Holmes reminded him.

'Liggett'll never let that happen,' Jesse said. 'And neither will I.'

Without another word he stormed off into the fog.

Watson fished out his cab whistle and said: 'Go after him, Holmes. I'll keep an eye on these two until the police get here. And Holmes?'

'Yes, Watson?'

'For God's sake, be careful.'

As Holmes dashed off into the mist, Watson blew the whistle three times in quick succession to summon the police.

★ ★ ★

Jesse rounded the corner, the only sound now the echo of his own hurried footsteps and the fading crackle of the burning coach. He searched the fog for signs of Liggett but saw nothing. He broke cover, moving cat-quick into the middle of the road, breath held, blood pounding in his ears.

Suddenly there was a muffled drumming of hoofs, a sense of something large coming fast out of the fog. Jesse threw himself sideways as Liggett, astride one of the carriage horses, came charging toward him. Man and horse thundered past. The horse's shoulder caught Jesse a glancing blow. He staggered back, firing off-balance into the billowing fog, then cursed, knowing he'd missed his target.

He heard the restless snicker of the other

horse somewhere behind him and hurried toward the sound. After about twenty or thirty paces he glimpsed it in the mist ahead. It stood motionless, unable to run any further because of the trailing reins wrapped around its hind legs.

'Easy, feller,' Jesse said soothingly. 'Easy . . . easy . . . ' He holstered his gun and slowly closed on the horse.

When he reached it he gently stroked its neck and used his clasp-knife to slice through the tangle of reins and buckles. He then grabbed a handful of the horse's mane and leapt astride. Wheeling the horse around, he was just about to dig his spurs in when a figure appeared out of the fog before him, waving his arms above his head — Holmes.

'Step aside!' Jesse yelled. 'Liggett's gettin' away!'

Holmes ran alongside the horse and extended his hand. 'Help me up.'

'You loco? We'll never catch him, ridin' double!'

'We go together or *you* don't go at all,' Holmes said firmly.

Jesse swore, but knew they didn't have time to argue. He grabbed Holmes's hand and pulled him up behind him. He then spurred the horse into a gallop and they rode blindly into the silent, swirling fog.

21

The Thames Tunnel

As they galloped through the night, in and out of patches of fog, Holmes tried to find his bearings. To his left the Thames lay oily and black, with yellow mist curling around all the ships at anchor. To his right tall warehouses reached up into the shrouding mist. Here was Pelican Wharf, then Gun Wharf, then Union Coal Wharf. And just as Holmes realized approximately where they were, there was a sudden break in the fog. Hearing the sound of hoof-beats coming towards them from the left, Jesse quickly reined up and dragged out his Peacemaker.

Moments later Liggett's horse trotted up — without its rider — and snorted when it recognized its stablemate.

Jesse and Holmes exchanged puzzled looks.

'Think he might've taken a fall?' asked Jesse.

'It's possible.'

'Then again, maybe he's just gone to ground, waitin' for a chance to hit us from cover.'

Holmes was listening to the night — to the *silent* night.

'I *knew* it!' Jesse hissed as his temper boiled over. 'The sonofabitch's given us the slip! Damn you, Holmes, I could've shot him if you hadn't — '

'Quiet!' interrupted Holmes. 'Listen . . . '

Jesse listened, but heard nothing save the distant sound of a train. 'What . . . ?'

Holmes turned and looked about him. At last, getting his bearings, he pointed ahead through the drifting, shroudlike haze: 'There!'

'Where?' Jesse said, squinting. 'All I see is some kind of buildin'. Looks like a church.'

It was an easy mistake to make. The structure was octagonal in shape, with a number of large doors and what appeared to be marble walls.

'It is not exactly a building,' Holmes corrected. 'It's actually the old pedestrian entrance to the Thames Tunnel.'

'What the hell's the Thames Tunnel?'

'It runs beneath the river and connects Wapping — where we are now — with Rotherhithe, on the far side.'

'An' you think Liggett's gone down there?'

'He would not have given up his horse otherwise,' said Holmes. 'There's nowhere else to go.'

'OK,' muttered Jesse. 'So let's go find us a sidewinder.'

He nudged the horse toward the tunnel entrance. It was even larger and more impressive close up. Keeping the horse at a walk, he guided the hesitant animal through one of the tall doors, on into a shadowy rotunda some fifty feet in diameter. The riderless horse followed docilely behind. Their hoofs clattered against the blue-and-white marble mosaic floor, the noise echoing off the stuccoed walls until they came to a halt. The damp, mouldy stink of the Thames flooded their senses.

Ahead, a sort of watch-house stood on the side of the rotunda closest to the river, beside which stood a broken, rusted brass turnstile. Wordlessly, Holmes slid from the horse's back and hopped nimbly over the gate. There was a door in the facing wall and he carefully pushed it open a crack.

Echoes drifted up to them — the sounds made by a man hurriedly descending a flight of stone steps.

Holmes and Jesse exchanged another look. Then Jesse leapt from the horse, vaulted the turnstile and the two men pushed through the door together.

Beyond lay a poorly lit circular shaft, with a now-dusty marble stairway that descended first to a gallery midway down, and then to a marble platform eighty feet below.

Racing headlong down the steps was Cage Liggett. He was almost at the bottom.

Jesse yelled: '*Liggett!*'

Liggett glanced up. In the gloom he looked pale as chalk, his eyes large and fearful. Pausing, he snapped off a shot at them.

The shot filled the shaft with echoes. Jesse pushed Holmes down even as the bullet dug into the wall behind them and plaster chips sprayed across their shoulders.

Jesse returned fire, but his bullet ricocheted off a baluster rail and whined harmlessly into the darkness.

Below, Liggett sprinted out of sight.

Jumping up, Jesse and Holmes gave chase. It was a dangerously steep descent but both men seemed oblivious to the prospect of a fall as they galloped downward in an effort to reach the platform below before Liggett eluded them entirely.

As they came off the bottom step they found themselves in a nearly exact copy of the rotunda above, equally poorly lit by infrequent, sputtering gas lamps. There were two once ornate arches in the back wall. Each led out into tunnels that were mirror-images of themselves. Each had a fourteen-foot wide road laid out with railway tracks and, beside it, an additional pedestrian walkway some three feet wide. Although the air was rank with drifting smoke, for there was little ventilation down here, Jesse felt as though he were in an underground cathedral. The tunnel was about twenty feet high, and close to forty feet wide. Each tunnel was supported by a series of ornate arches. The lighting was poor, the shadows deep, and Jesse sensed that unseen eyes were watching them — and not just those of Cage Liggett.

In the next moment Holmes confirmed it. 'Have a care, Mr James. This was once the eighth wonder of the world, a thoroughfare for pedestrian and carriage alike.'

'What happened?'

'When it failed to draw sufficient customers it was sold to the East London Railway and is now used for the transporting of goods from one side of the river to the other. But it is also home for an entire sub-culture of thieves and vagabonds, who will cut your throat just to see the colour of your — '

Another shot roared along the tunnel, making both men flatten themselves against the wall. Before the echo faded Jesse leapt into the tunnel and returned fire.

Liggett was already forty yards away and running as fast as he could. Jesse's bullet clipped one of the arches just beyond him, barely missing his head, forcing Liggett to veer off the walkway on to the railway tracks.

Jesse sprinted after him, his alternately shrinking and stretching shadow keeping pace with him on the grimy left-side wall.

Holmes chased after them, but hadn't gone far when he realized that the traverse arches that separated the twin tunnels were littered with crude, unmade cribs, cooking-fires, a pathetic scattering of personal possessions — and people.

Alerted by the exchange of gunfire, a group of them now shuffled out of the darkness ahead. Some carried flaming torches and held them up in an effort to see what was causing the shooting. Backs to Holmes, they blocked his path, giving him no choice but to stop or run into them.

'Who was that?'

'What's goin' on?'

'Can you see 'im?'

'I can! See! It's a bloke wiv a gun!'

'Two blokes wiv guns — look!'

Then one of them glanced round and noticed Holmes standing behind them.

''Ere! Who're you?'

As one, they all turned and looked at Holmes.

'I bet 'e's wiv them other two . . . '

''Cept 'e don't 'ave no gun!'

Suddenly Holmes became the focus of their unwelcome attention, and the sight of so many grubby, misshapen wretches shuffling menacingly toward him chilled even his brave soul. Most of them were men in rags, the faces below their overlarge caps smudged and dirty, the whites of their eyes a sickly yellow, their teeth, as they leered at him, broken, badly discoloured or missing altogether.

The women were no better. They wore tattered shawls, and their soot-stained skin was equally raddled. Holmes's eyes widened with horror as he saw that one of them was cradling a baby, saw that these poor souls didn't just live in this anteroom to hell, they raised babies here as well.

But he realized that this was no time for misplaced sentiment. Life for these poor unfortunates was pure drudgery, and he knew they would grab at any opportunity, legal or otherwise, to improve their lot — even if it meant committing murder.

Drawing himself up to his full height, he ordered those bunched in front of him to step aside.

They made no attempt to obey him.

'You heard me,' Holmes cried tightly. 'Get out of my way!'

'An' if we don't?' someone said. 'What'll *you* do 'bout it, eh?'

'Just 'cause yer one a them rich toffs,' another said, 'don't give you the right to come down 'ere and tell us what to do.'

An ugly chorus of 'ayes' arose from the crowd.

Holmes pulled down a breath of stale, heated air. 'I'm not trying to tell you or your companions anything,' he said. 'But you have to let me pass so that I — '

His voice was drowned out by the shouts coming from the angry men and women around him. Their dirty, pallid faces were sullen and belligerent with resentment. Some of them cursed Holmes; others pressed forward menacingly.

One of the men nearest Holmes pulled a knife from under his threadbare jacket and waved it threateningly in Holmes's face. He was so close that Holmes could smell his malodorous breath, could see that his right eye had filmed over and was the colour of sour milk.

'All right, guv'nor,' the man snarled. 'You wanna come down 'ere, you gots to pay the price of admission! 'And over yer wallet!'

Before Holmes could decide what to do, another gun-blast echoed along the tunnel, causing the baby to cry. Holmes, aware that other men and women had appeared behind him and that he was in danger of being surrounded, dug out his wallet and threw it off to his right, over the heads of the crowd.

'There,' he said, adding: 'Now let me pass!'

Even as he spoke both groups broke apart and went in search of the wallet, cursing and punching each other as they scurried back into the shadows.

Seeing his chance, Holmes did something he'd never done in his life before: he fled.

★   ★   ★

Further ahead in the tunnel Jesse was slowly gaining on Liggett. Realizing that he was about to get caught, Liggett abruptly turned and fired. The bullet barely missed Jesse, ricocheting off the wall near his head and whining down the tunnel. Without breaking stride Jesse drew his Colt, took quick aim and fired twice.

Liggett grunted, staggered on for a few steps and then collapsed on the tracks.

It's done, Jesse thought, hardly able to believe it. *It's over. Finished.*

Chest heaving, he walked slowly up to the body.

Cage Liggett lay on his belly, face turned sideways, left cheek pressed against the ballast packed tight between each tie of the railway. Jesse looked down at him for an instant, almost disappointed that in the end, his enemy's death had come so quick and easy.

His thoughts turned briefly to Ma, and Archie. He thought of Frank and . . .

Liggett rolled over, gun in hand, and pulled the trigger.

Jesse lurched backward, mentally cursing himself for not realizing that Liggett had been faking, and felt the burn of the bullet as it creased his left arm and ricocheted off the roof.

Liggett swore and went to fire again.

Simultaneously, Jesse aimed his own gun at Liggett and fired.

Both triggers clicked on empty chambers.

For an infinitesimal moment each man froze, realizing he was out of lead.

Then Liggett hurled his empty gun at Jesse and scrambled to his feet. Jesse charged him, months of pent-up rage erupting with all the violence of a volcano. He slammed Liggett against the wall and tried to strangle him. For several moments the two men grappled, each struggling to get the upper hand. Then, Liggett managed to knee Jesse in the groin. As Jesse doubled over in pain, Liggett clasped his hands together and brought them down on the back of Jesse's head, smashing him on to the tracks. Before Jesse could recover, Liggett started kicking him in the ribs.

Desperately, Jesse grabbed Liggett's ankles and jerked him off his feet. Liggett went down in a heap. Jesse was on him immediately, straddling him, hitting him again and again.

But Liggett wasn't done yet. Bringing his legs up, he wrapped them around Jesse's neck and jerked him backward. Jesse's head thudded against a tarnished rail. Momentarily stunned, he felt Liggett's legs increase the pressure about his neck. Unable to breath, Jesse started to black out. Desperately he tried to break the stranglehold. It was impossible.

Though he fought it as much as he could, he began to lose consciousness. In a last frantic attempt to escape, he twisted to his left, at the same time violently kicking his legs. The move unseated Liggett. He fell sideways, his face hitting one of the ties. But he was up again quickly, threatening Jesse with Blackrat's distinctive horn-handle knife.

'Come on, then!' he screamed, blood running from his nose on to his handlebar moustache. 'Let's finish this once and for — '

Jesse kicked the knife from Liggett's hand. It flipped end over end and landed on the left side of the tracks, the blade wedged under the rail. Liggett dived for it, grasped the handle and pulled. Nothing happened. He tugged harder but the blade wouldn't break free. Hearing Jesse closing in on him, Liggett desperately forced his hand under the track and tried to pull the knife loose.

It wouldn't budge. He tried harder. But the knife still wouldn't move. Worse, Liggett realized his hand was now stuck between the bottom of the rail and the ballast under it.

He heard Jesse's boots crunching closer, looked up and saw the man from Missouri standing over him.

'Give it up,' Jesse growled. 'It's over.'

Liggett spat at him and made one final effort to pull his hand loose. When that failed he said: 'Go ahead, then, you sonofabitch. Shoot me.'

'I'd like to,' Jesse said. 'More'n anythin'. But I gave my word to Holmes and I never break my word. You're goin' back home to hang for what you done to Ma and — '

He broke off as he heard a rumbling in the distance.

Liggett heard it too.

A train was coming.

Liggett became saucer-eyed with fear. Panicking, he struggled to pull his hand loose. When it wouldn't come, he begged: 'Help me, Jesse! Help me!'

Jesse heard the train coming closer and felt the ground tremble underfoot.

'Sorry,' he said coldly. 'I gave my word not to shoot you. But I never said I'd help save your life.'

'Jesse, for God's sake,' Liggett pleaded. 'You can't let me die like this!'

'Archie never asked to die the way he did, either. But that didn't keep it from happenin'.'

The rumble of the approaching train was louder now. And the trembling of the ground increased.

Liggett saw the cold, flinty look in Jesse's light blue eyes and knew he was a dead man. Teeth gritted, he continued trying to pull his hand free. It was hopeless.

He closed his eyes and started blubbering.

'Damn you!' Jesse said. Kneeling beside Liggett, he grabbed his arm and pulled. Nothing happened. He pulled again, hard as he could. Again, nothing.

Just then the headlight of the fast-moving train came sweeping around a curve in the tracks. It flooded over the two men.

Liggett screamed for Jesse to help him. Jesse tried frantically to pull the hand loose, but it was impossible.

He jumped to his feet and stood in the middle of the tracks, waving his hands for the oncoming train to stop.

But the driver didn't even see him and the squat, ugly-snouted locomotive continued to thunder down on them, smoke from its stack flattening out against the tunnel roof and then spilling back down the soot-stained sides like ink spiralling through water.

'Get me out of here!' Liggett blubbered. 'For God's sake, Jesse, please, I'm beggin'!'

But it was too late.

The onrushing train barrelled toward them, hauling a long line of produce-filled freight wagons behind it.

Jesse, realizing he couldn't even *hope* to save Liggett, went to step off the tracks.

Before he could, Liggett's free hand grabbed Jesse's ankle and jerked him off his feet.

'If I'm gonna die,' he hissed, 'you're comin' with me, you pig-suckin' Confederate bastard!'

Jesse tried to pull free, but Liggett had a death grip on his ankle.

The train thundered closer, almost on them now.

Jesse desperately kicked Liggett in the face, but the onetime Pinkerton grimly held on.

This was how it ended, then. Liggett would die, but so would he.

Then two hands grabbed him by the

shoulders and jerked him backward, freeing him from Liggett's grasp. Jesse quickly rolled over on the ground, to the safety of the narrow pedestrian walkway.

An instant later the train thundered over the spot he had just occupied.

The spot Liggett *still* occupied.

His ungodly, agonizing scream was lost in the roar of the speeding train.

Jesse, heart thudding, turned and found himself staring Holmes in the face.

The train was making too much noise for Jesse to be heard, but Holmes was able to lip-read the single word:

'*Thanks.*'

22

The Queen of Diamonds

By the time Watson and the police arrived, Jesse had faded into the mist. Neither he nor Holmes made any reference to the man from Missouri in their subsequent statements. Acting upon the information they *did* supply, however, the police quickly descended upon the Poacher's Pocket and obtained the names of Desmond O'Leary and Olwenyo Wadlock from the landlord. Both were well-known to the men of K Division, and were arrested at their lodgings within the hour. They were charged with the robbery of the City branch of Crosbie & Shears, and by the time the police finished searching their rooms, along with those of Alfie Adams and the barge upon which Cage and Jack Liggett had been living, most of the stolen money was recovered.

Jesse emerged from the shadows as Holmes and Watson came out of Bow Road police station and the three men went in search of a cab. It took a while, even with Watson blowing his cab-whistle at regular intervals, and by the time they all eventually returned to Montague Hall it was well after midnight.

The ride in the cab was a quiet one. Though there was obviously plenty to talk about, words seemed inadequate to describe all that had happened and none of them was willing to break the silence.

Elaina was waiting up for them in the sitting room. When she saw Jesse's bruised and battered condition she threw herself unashamedly into his arms. Although he, Holmes and Watson were exhausted from the events of the evening, she insisted that they celebrate the end of Jesse's vengeance-quest with a glass of champagne, and asked Fordham to fetch a bottle from the cellar.

When their glasses were filled, she toasted: 'To friends . . . coming back safely.'

Jesse and Watson raised their glasses to drink, but Holmes, whose attention was focused on the champagne bottle, had other ideas. 'To diamonds,' he remarked softly.

Elaina gave him an odd look and for a moment seemed disconcerted. But she quickly regained her composure and, fingering the diamond necklace at her throat, smiled and said: 'Why, Holmes, what a splendid idea! I'll drink to diamonds any day.'

'Even the ones hidden in your wine cellar?' he asked.

For once Elaina was caught off guard. 'I beg your pardon?'

'Though it was wiped prior to serving,' Holmes explained, 'there is still a fine patina of *Erysiphacae* — more commonly known as powdery mildew — to be seen upon this champagne bottle.'

Elaina gave a nervous little laugh. 'Forgive me,' she said. 'I'll speak to Fordham. It will never happen again, I assure you.'

'You miss my point,' Holmes continued doggedly. 'Your cellar is damp, Countess, due no doubt to the Hall's close proximity to the Thames.'

Again Elaina laughed nervously. 'What's that got to do with anything?'

'Merely that I observe smudges of exactly the same mildew upon the hem of your dress, and also upon the heel of Mr James's right boot. My feeling is that having taken Mr James into your confidence, you have perhaps already shown him your ill-gotten collection of jewels . . . in the cellar?'

'Cellar?' she stalled. 'I don't under — '

'Inspector Rosier is already on his way,' Holmes went on bleakly. 'If you'd prefer, Countess, we can wait until he arrives before you hand them over.'

She feigned puzzlement. 'Hand *what* over? Holmes, I've no idea what you're talking ab — '

'Lady Darlington-Whit's teardrop earrings,' he snapped. 'The gold diamond pendant belonging to Baroness Alcott. Countess Broughton's pearl bracelet. Lady Bingham's mourning necklace ... and of course, the Star of Persia, which Mr James so kindly stole for you not twenty-four hours since.'

'That's a lie!' Elaina said, scandalized. 'I think you'd better leave — *now!*'

'If it's all the same to you, Countess,' Watson said politely, 'we shall await the arrival of Inspector Rosier.'

Elaina turned to Jesse. 'Aren't you going to *do* something?'

'Like, what?' he asked.

Elaina looked at Holmes, at Watson, then at Jesse again. Her deep topaz eyes suddenly hardened. '*Kill* them,' she hissed.

Watson drew a sharp breath.

'You sure 'bout that?' Jesse said. 'I mean, Holmes is a friend of yours, ain't he?'

'A 'friend' who intends to hand me over to Scotland Yard,' Elaina said bitterly. Then: 'Do it. Now!'

Jesse studied her for a long beat and then went to the portrait of Rupert Montague hanging beside the fireplace. He unhooked it to reveal the wall-safe behind and deftly worked the combination.

Elaina stared at him, wondering how he could possibly have known the combination, until she remembered that he had been refreshing his drink when she'd opened the safe earlier that evening; he must have watched her reflection in the mirror.

Jesse took out the derringer and tossed it to her. 'Here . . . '

'What's this for?'

'Ellie, I don't mean to sound ungrateful,' he drawled, 'but I reckon it's time you did your own dirty work.'

Elaina looked at the weapon and a strange, twisted smile tightened her lips. He was testing her, she realized, making sure she really had what it took to be an outlaw's mate. Well, that was just fine. He certainly wouldn't find her wanting.

'Gladly,' she said. She aimed the tiny gun at Holmes, adding: 'I really didn't want it to come to this, but you've left me no choice.'

Watson quickly stepped in front her target. 'No!'

Touched by his loyalty, Holmes reached out and gently forced him aside. 'Thanks, dear friend. But it will not be necessary.' Then to Elaina: 'This is not the first time you have taken a life, is it?'

'What do you mean?'

'The rumours are correct, are they not? You

did kill your husband.'

Her jaw clenched. 'You know better than that. It was an accident, plain and simple.'

'Come now, Countess,' Holmes mocked, 'Give me more credit than that.'

'Scotland Yard believed me. So did the coroner's office.'

'They had little choice,' put in Watson. 'There was no evidence to support the alternative.'

'Until now,' Holmes said.

'What do you mean?' Elaina said uneasily.

'At the request of Sir Ashley Danvers-Cole, and latterly the Commissioner of Police of the Metropolis, Lieutenant-Colonel Sir Edmund Henderson, I have been keeping a very close eye upon you, Countess, for one very specific reason. Since we could not arrest you for the murder of your husband, which we knew full well you had committed, we resolved to bide our time and make sure we could arrest and prosecute you quite successfully for the next crime you committed. All we were waiting for was the evidence.'

'You're bluffing,' Elaina said, not as convincingly as she'd intended.

'There's an easy way to find out,' Jesse said. 'Give him your gun. If you're innocent, like you claim, you got nothin' to worry about.'

''Cept to lose everything I've got.' She gave

an ugly laugh. 'No, thanks, gentlemen. I've worked too hard, eaten too much crow, taken too many risks to end up behind bars.' She turned back to Holmes, the derringer aimed at his chest. 'You're right, as usual. The earl was a means to an end. That's all he ever was to me.'

'And Mr James, here? He was a means to an end, too, wasn't he? The only man with nerve enough even to *attempt* the theft of the Star of Persia.'

Elaina did not say anything, but her silence condemned her.

'But what happens now that he too has reached the end of his usefulness? Can he expect the same fate as the earl?'

The derringer in Elaina's hand wavered and lowered a little. Her lips were tight but tremulous. She was, Holmes thought, a woman trying to summon the strength to pull the trigger; a woman unable to, a woman in defeat.

But he was wrong.

In the next instant she raised the little gun and pulled the trigger, causing Holmes and Watson to flinch instinctively.

The room was filled with a soft, metallic *click*!

Elaina quickly pulled the trigger again.

And again: *click*!

She stared at the derringer as if it had betrayed her.

Then she heard a clinking sound and, looking up, saw Jesse toying with the two shells in his free hand.

'Sorry, Ellie,' he said.

'*What?*'

'I emptied the gun right after Holmes called on you last night — when I offered to hang the portrait back for you.'

'B-But, *why?*'

''Cause I ain't the fool you played me for.'

'Jesse, darling, I never thought — '

'Holmes wasn't tellin' me anythin' I didn't already know,' he continued sourly. 'It's like Frank's always sayin': Beautiful women like you are the same everywhere. And believe me I've known more'n my share. You find a feller, take whatever it is you want from him and then cast him loose — or, in your case, push him down a flight of stairs.'

'Why, that's utter nonsense,' Elaina began.

Jesse stopped her. 'The moment I agreed to steal that diamond for you, I knew it was only a matter of time before you took care of me, too.'

Holmes relaxed and gave a brief tic of a smile. 'I obviously underestimated you, Mr James.'

'You ain't the first.'

'And probably not the last,' Holmes said, adding: 'Shall we go down to the cellar, then, and collect the evidence?'

'Thought you'd never get around to it,' Jesse said. He looked at the countess. 'Lead the way . . . *Ellie*.'

23

Escape!

Elaina grudgingly led them down to the cellar. At the bottom of the steps, she raised the gas, illuminating the secret door that concealed the small, damp room beyond. For a moment no one moved. There was only silence. Then Holmes spotted the candle and matches on the shelf just inside the darkened doorway and entering, quickly brought light to the scene. As he held the candle up, casting flickering shadows on the walls, Jesse and Watson entered and started to examine the treasure-filled display case more closely.

Watching them from the doorway Elaina said proudly: 'It's quite something, isn't it, gentlemen?'

'Indeed it is,' observed Watson. 'All that's missing is the crown jewels.'

'Too ostentatious, even for me,' she said, smiling.

Jesse grunted. 'I'll believe that, Ellie, when they build a bank too big to rob.'

Elaine laughed, but it was difficult to tell

whether it was bravado or that she really did believe she would get out of this. Confronting the three men, she said brazenly: 'It's not too late to work something out, you know. The earl left me well very provided for. There's more than enough to go around.'

Jesse shook his head, amazed by her gall. 'Looks like I ain't the only outlaw you know, Holmes.'

'Quite.'

'Well,' Elaina said, 'you can't blame a girl for trying.'

'Holmes, look,' Watson pointed. 'Isn't that the Star of Persia?'

Holmes nodded. 'It must be, old friend. There cannot be two gems of *that* magnitude on this earth.' He turned back to Elaina, ready to chide her for almost causing a serious international incident — but she was gone.

Jesse realized it at the same instant. 'What the hell — ?'

Holmes pushed past him, back out into the cellar. In the opposite wall another secret door stood ajar, the passage beyond it dark as pitch. 'This way!' he shouted. He ran toward it, his free hand cupped around the flickering candle flame to keep it from blowing out.

Jesse followed him through the opening, Watson limping behind.

The unlighted tunnel was damp, winding and narrow. Originally dug by river pirates and smugglers, in most parts it was barely wide enough for one person to pass through. The ceiling was low and uneven, as if the excavating had been careless and rushed.

As the three of them ran they had to duck to avoid hitting their heads on the jagged protrusions. The tunnel twisted one way, then another, until at last Holmes felt a draught of cool night air on his face and picked up the pace.

'We're almost to the end,' he called back to the others.

'Thank God for that,' said Watson as he laboured along.

As they rounded another bend, an opening appeared ahead. It was narrower than the tunnel and Watson groaned as he saw it. The last in line, he watched as first Holmes then Jesse crawled through.

Outside, standing amid a tangle of brush, Holmes said urgently: 'Come on! We have to stop the countess from escaping!'

'I'm right behind you,' said Jesse. Together the three of them fought their way through the dense patch of bushes, roots and weeds that tried to trip them at every step. Eventually they clawed their way free and found themselves on the mud-caked, moonlit banks of the Thames.

They looked in all directions but could see no movement.

'She can't've gotten too far ahead,' Jesse said.

'Don't be too sure,' Holmes replied. 'The lady's running for her very life. You of all people should understand how desperate she'll be to avoid prison or worse.' He broke off suddenly and pointed toward the river. 'There she is!'

Jesse squinted into the semi-darkness and saw an indistinct figure climbing into a rowing boat some fifty yards downriver. Beyond, a bank of dense fog loomed ominously.

'Damn,' he said. 'She'll be mid-stream 'fore we reach her.'

'That depends on how good a shot you are,' remarked Holmes.

Jesse frowned at him. 'I ain't much on killin' women,' he growled.

'Blast it, man. I meant the rowing boat.'

Jesse grinned. 'Just testin' you, brother.' He drew one of his Colts and took careful aim at the little boat — now pulling away from the bank as Elaina tugged on the oars.

'Be sure to aim below the waterline,' Holmes said.

Jesse started to squeeze the trigger. But at

that moment a swell lifted the rowing boat, putting Elaina square in the sights. Jesse stopped squeezing, re-aimed at the bobbing boat and fired.

The boom of the big Colt shattered the silent darkness. A miniature water spout spurted up about a foot from the bow of the moving boat.

Elaine immediately looked back at them, and rowed even faster toward the fog bank.

'Your skills as a marksman appear to have deserted you, all of a sudden,' noted Holmes sourly.

Jesse gave him a sidelong glance, the meaning of which was almost impossible to read in the misty darkness. 'It's been a long night,' he replied.

He snatched his other Colt from its holster and fired on the move. This time there was no water spout. A moment later the rowing boat lurched to the left and slowly began to sink.

Holmes hurried off along the riverbank, Watson at his heels. Jesse holstered his guns and loped after them. When they reached the spot from where Elaina had launched the rowing boat, they realized their chase was over. Though listing badly, the craft was still afloat, and Elaina's steady rowing had brought her to the edge of the fog bank.

'Well,' Holmes said irritably, 'unless you

wish to indulge in a cold midnight swim, I fear the countess has eluded us. Perhaps permanently.'

'You go ahead,' Jesse said. 'Me, I've never been partial to water.'

Frustrated, the three men watched as Elaina rested one oar and mockingly blew them a kiss. Then she went back to rowing and within moments the little boat vanished into the fog.

'You gotta admit,' Jesse chuckled, 'the lady has grit.'

'Or the devil's own luck,' murmured Watson.

Jesse grinned. 'Reckon my brother Frank was right. He always said the difference 'tween a dead fox an' a smart fox is that a smart fox always digs two holes — one to come in, one to sneak out.'

'Your brother,' said Watson, fishing out a handkerchief to mop his sweated brow, 'sounds like a jolly wise man.'

24

A Fresh Start

The London and North Western Railway station at Euston echoed to the sounds of the Liverpool train preparing to depart. Peering down at Holmes and Watson from an open carriage window, Jesse said: 'Well, this is it, I reckon. And by the looks on your faces, it ain't a moment too soon.'

Two days had passed since Elaina disappeared into the fog. Nothing had been seen of her since, despite a nationwide search for her whereabouts.

'Well, you must admit, things have been rather hectic of late,' said Watson, smiling. 'I for one intend to spend a few days doing nothing more exciting than perusing my stamp collection.'

'Beats watching corn grow,' Jesse said. 'You ever come to Missoura, Doc, you can ride with me'n Frank any time.'

'I appreciate that, old chap,' said Watson. They shook hands firmly.

When it was Holmes's turn, he deliberately

held on to Jesse's hand and looked him directly in the eyes. 'This is none of my business, of course,' he said, 'but I don't suppose you'd consider following a different, ah, 'calling' upon your return to the colonies?'

'I don't suppose I would,' Jesse said.

'Even though the life of an outlaw has already cost you so dearly?'

Jesse shrugged. 'That's the thing about 'the life of an outlaw', as you call it. It might be hell, but the money's good and the hours are short.'

'I won't argue with you there,' Holmes said. 'Good luck, then, Mr James, and God speed.'

'Same to you, Holmes.'

The blast of a whistle echoed shrilly through the station, making an elderly, grey-haired lady who had been shuffling along the platform hurriedly clamber aboard.

Holmes and Watson stood back. Jesse offered them one final wave, then closed the window and went to find a seat.

The train was already leaving the station by the time he entered a compartment that was empty save for the elderly woman, who was now dozing. He stowed his luggage in the overhead net and flopped down on to the opposite seat.

The train gathered speed and was soon

gently rocking along. As Jesse watched the passing scenery — mostly soot-blackened brick walls and the backs of tenement houses — he thought about everything that had happened during his visit to England. It was just as Watson had said. The dull moments had been few and far between.

The long voyage home, however, promised to be just the opposite.

On the way here he'd had his thoughts of revenge to occupy him. To kill time, he must have dreamed up a dozen different ways to settle the account with Cage and Jack Liggett. But now that the brothers were dead, what else did he have to think about, except returning home to his old ways? And though he looked forward to seeing Frank and their mother, and maybe a woman or two, the thought of robbing trains and banks no longer seemed as exciting as it once had.

The elderly woman dozing opposite him suddenly stirred and appeared to wake up. She peered at him through small, wire-framed spectacles and said hesitantly: 'Excuse me. Is that *you*, Mr Howard?'

He frowned at her. 'Do I know you, ma'am?'

'Oh, I think so,' said Elaina. She sat up a little straighter, and after looking around to make sure no one was likely to see her, took off her glasses and grey wig.

Jesse's mouth dropped. 'Jesus on the cross,' he said softly.

Elaina chuckled. 'Nice to see you again, Jesse.' Then as he stared at her, lost for words: 'I wasn't really going to shoot you, you know.'

'Like hell you weren't.'

'Well, maybe just a friendly nick. Anyway, you're no innocent yourself.'

Jesse raised his eyebrows. 'Ma'am?'

'Were you aiming at me that night, or my boat?' she asked bluntly.

He showed her a huge grin. 'I guess we'll never know, will we?'

She matched his smile. 'Well, let's just say we're even, then.'

Still unable to believe her gall, Jesse said: 'You *do* know they're turnin' this country upside down, searchin' for you?'

'Let them,' she replied. 'Bumbling fools. I won't be here much longer.'

'Oh? Where you goin'?'

'I thought perhaps Missoura.'

'Missoura?'

'Yes. Kearney, maybe.'

'Thinkin' of makin' a fresh start?'

'Why not? Thanks to Sherlock Holmes, I now find myself right back where I started — at the bottom.'

'I doubt you'll stay there long,' Jesse predicted.

'Let's hope not. I've experienced both the bottom and the top, and there's no doubt the top is better.'

'Couldn't agree more. And if ever I can help, be sure'n let me know.'

'Does that mean you don't mind me tagging along, Mr Howard?'

Rising, he went and sat next to her. 'I don't mind in the *least*, Miss Corbin.'

★   ★   ★

As they left the station and Holmes stepped out on to the pavement to hail a passing hansom, Watson said: 'I was just thinking. Do you suppose we'll ever see the countess again?'

'I would not be at all surprised,' Holmes replied. He smiled, remembering the old grey-haired lady on the platform. 'But if we *do*, then I rather suspect that she will have swapped her petticoats for leather chaps and spurs.'

We do hope that you have enjoyed reading this large print book.

Did you know that all of our titles are available for purchase?

We publish a wide range of high quality large print books including:
Romances, Mysteries, Classics
General Fiction
Non Fiction and Westerns

Special interest titles available in large print are:
The Little Oxford Dictionary
Music Book
Song Book
Hymn Book
Service Book

Also available from us courtesy of Oxford University Press:
Young Readers' Dictionary
(large print edition)
Young Readers' Thesaurus
(large print edition)

For further information or a free brochure, please contact us at:
Ulverscroft Large Print Books Ltd.,
The Green, Bradgate Road, Anstey,
Leicester, LE7 7FU, England.
Tel: (00 44) 0116 236 4325
Fax: (00 44) 0116 234 0205

Other titles published by
The House of Ulverscroft:

FAMILY FALLOUT

Peter Conway

Alex, the sixteen-year-old adopted daughter of Tory MP Richard Travers, is found drowned with a head injury in a pond, in the garden of her family home in Oxfordshire. With the local police force short-handed, two detectives from Scotland Yard investigate what is — they soon discover — a seriously dysfunctional family. Alex had been difficult to manage and Madeleine, the MP's wife, had religious beliefs that convinced her and her eighteen-year-old son, Matthew, that Alex was evil. Only Alex's widowed maternal grandmother could handle her, which then leads to further strife within the family — until the final shocking truth is revealed.